Born to Serve

(Cover image: "Maiden Picking Flowers," by American artist, Daniel Ridgway Knight, 1890.)

Born to Serve

The Legacy of Home Press Classic Edition

by Charles M. Sheldon

The text from the current edition was carefully transcribed and lightly edited from the 1900 edition, originally published by:
Advance Publishing Company, Chicago, U.S.A.

Any additional images or text that has been added includes their source.

All Scripture Quotations are from the King James Bible.

ISBN Number: 978-1-956616-21-7

The Legacy of Home Press

Vermont - U.S.A.

Foreword

THIS book is part of a series we are republishing for our Classic Book Collection. It is fascinating in its description of domestic life and the difficulty of obtaining hired help for the home.

The main character, Barbara, is a recent college graduate who is living at home with her widowed mother. She is unable to find a job and decides to take a position as a "hired-girl" in a private home. Her work involves managing the house, taking care of children, cooking, and cleaning. She becomes very dear to the family she works for as she makes their home comfortable and pleasant with her faithful and skilled labor.

The work of a hired-girl, however, is considered to be only for those of the lower class. House work is thought of as drudgery and looked down upon by society. Barbara is troubled by the glaring difference in the manner of which the working class is treated compared to the wealthy. Most of the hired-girls don't care about their work. They are inefficient and unskilled, making home life miserable and stressful for their employers. An idea is formulated to start a housekeeping school to train the workers.

This wholesome story provides an interesting look at what life was like in the early 1900's. Readers will appreciate old time Christian values and morals from a different era.

It is refreshing to read about their family worship, prayer, and church attendance. A gentle, old fashioned romance develops which is inspiring.

The overall theme presents a beautiful message of the blessing of living one's life in service to the Lord.

Mrs. Sharon White
- The Legacy of Home Press -
Vermont, 2023.

Contents

Preface by the Author

This little story, "Born to Serve," was written with the purpose of calling attention to a real question, not with any purpose of attempting a solution of the problem.

If the story serves its purpose in simply emphasizing in the minds of all who labor, the religious side of all human service, I shall count the task well worth all it has cost.

Charles M. Sheldon

Central Church, Topeka, Kansas.

Born to Serve

CHAPTER 1

The World Needs Love.

"AT the same time, Richard," said Mrs. Richard Ward anxiously, "it comes back to the old question, 'What are we to do?' You know I am not strong enough to keep house alone. We can't afford to break up our home and go into a hotel, and yet it seems almost the only thing left to do. What shall we do?"

"I don't understand why all our girls stay so short a time!" exclaimed Mr. Ward irritably. And then he looked across the table at his wife, and his look softened a little as he noted more carefully her tired face and the traces of tears on her cheeks.

"Oh, I don't understand it! All I know is that they are all simply horrid. I do everything for them and never get anything but ingratitude from every one of them! The idea of Maggie leaving me today of all the days, just when Aunt Wilson was coming, Arthur home from college, and Lewis down with his accident; it is more than I can bear, Richard. If you were any sort of a man, you would know what to do!"

"Well, I am any sort of a man, and I don't know in the least what to do," replied Mr. Richard Ward to himself, as his wife laid her head down on the table regardless of several dishes overturned, and broke into sobs as a relief to her feelings which had been growing in hysterical power ever since Maggie, the hired-girl, had that morning not only given notice of her departure, but had actually left, after a brief but heated discussion about the housework in the Ward family.

The two children at the table turned frightened looks first at the father and then at the mother, and the youngest of them began to cry.

"Stop that, Carl!" exclaimed Mr. Ward sharply. Then, as he pushed back his plate with the food on it untouched, he muttered to himself: "I'm losing all my Christianity over this miserable hired-girl business. It's breaking up our home life and wrecking the joy of our very children."

The child's lip curled in a piteous effort at control and the older one began eating again, looking to father and mother anxiously.

Mr. Ward rose, and, going over to his wife, he sat down by her and stroked her head gently.

"There, Martha, you are all worn out. Just go into the sitting-room and lie down. George and I will do up the dishes, won't we, George? We'll play hired-girl tonight, won't we?"

"Let me help, too!" cried Carl.

"Yes, you can help, too. Finish your supper, and we'll have a jolly time washing and wiping. Now, Martha, you go in and lie down. We'll get things straightened out somehow."

Mrs. Ward feebly protested, but allowed her husband to lead her into the sitting-room, where she sank down on a lounge.

"I've got a splitting headache, Richard; leave the dishes until morning. You're tired with your business."

"No, I don't like to see them lying around. Besides, dirty dishes have a way of growing with miraculous rapidity when the girl's gone and things go to pieces like this," he said with a lapse into irritation again.

"It's not my fault!" exclaimed Mrs. Ward sharply. "Carl, stop that noise," she added as Carl began to gather up some of the dishes, piling the biggest plates on the little ones and letting several knives and forks clatter to the floor in his eagerness to help.

"Don't be always nagging the children, Martha!" said Mr. Ward angrily, losing his temper for the tenth time that evening. The other times he had lost it silently.

"It's always, 'Stop that noise!' from mother when her head aches," said George as he tried to pick up the knives and forks quietly, and let them drop twice before he had them back on the table.

"See me help! See me help!" sung Carl as he started towards the kitchen door with his arms full of dishes. The pile was too heavy for his strength; and, as he neared the door the column began to topple, it balanced for a moment on the edge of safety, and then fell with a crash. The child looked at the ruin a moment in terrified silence, then sat down on the floor and began to cry.

Mrs. Ward sat up on the lounge and looked at her husband almost savagely.

"Richard Ward, if you don't do something to change all this –"

She did not finish her sentence, but lay down and turned her face to the wall in despair. And Richard Ward, of the firm of Mead, Ward, and Company, known in business circles as a good, agreeable, and fairly successful merchant, and in church circles as a consistent member and active Christian man, turned from his wife and went out into the dining-room with a look on his face that his minster had never seen, and a feeling in his heart that was a good way from being what might be expected in a man who was "in good and regular standing" in the Marble Square Church.

"It would be very funny, if it were not so near a tragedy," he said to himself as he picked up the broken dishes while the two boys looked on. "It would be comical, if it were not so miserably serious in its effects on our home life. Here I am doing the dirty, common work of the kitchen. I, Richard Ward, the dignified, well-to-do member of the firm of Mead, Ward, and Company, all because of this girl, who –"

He did not finish the sentence even to himself but went on with the work of clearing the table, making the two boys sit down in a corner of the dining-room while he did the work. When he had carried everything out, he let the children go out into the kitchen with him, while he carefully shut the door into the dining-room and then proceeded to "do up" the dishes, letting George help, and finally, in answer to the younger boy's plea, allowing him to carry some of the indestructible dishes into the pantry.

"It's fun, isn't it, papa?" said Carl, as the last dish was wiped and the towels hung up.

"Great fun," replied Mr. Ward grimly.

"Father means it isn't," said George with superior wisdom.

"Anyhow, I think it's fun. Only I don't like the old girls. They make mamma feel bad. Do they make you feel bad, papa?"

"Yes, my son, they do," replied Mr. Ward as he sat down in one of the old kitchen chairs and took his younger son into his lap. And, if the truth were told, if his two small sons had not been present, it is possible Mr. Richard Ward might actually have shed tears over the constantly recurring tragedy of the "hired girl" as it had been acted in various forms in his own household during the last five years since they had moved into the city and his wife's health begun to break down from household cares.

"And yet I don't understand these women," he said to himself as he sat there in the kitchen, his chin on the little boy's head, while George perched on the kitchen table gravely observant. "We have everything in the world to do with. Our family is not very large. Martha is kind, and gives the girls very many favors. We pay good wages and are ready to put up with many kinds of incompetency, and yet we don't seem to be able to keep any sort of a girl more than three months at a time. It is breaking up our home life. It is simply absurd that I should be doing this kitchen work, but Martha isn't well, and there's breakfast to get and all the work after it."

He thought of his wife in the other room on the lounge, and was filled with remorse for her.

"I was a brute to talk to her so sharply," he said out loud.

"Brutes don't talk," said George from his elevated post on the table, speaking from knowledge gained in a study of a natural-history primer given him by his Aunt Wilson.

"Some of them do. The two-legged ones," replied his father. And then he rose, and with the boys went into the sitting-room.

They found that Mrs. Ward had gone upstairs in answer to a call from Lewis, the oldest boy of the family at home, who had broken his arm the week before while engaged in sport at school.

The duty of putting the two younger lads to bed devolved upon the father. He performed the duty without much heart in it. His wife was silent and in no mood for reconciliation. When Carl said his usual prayer, he added, "And bless Maggie, because she is so bad, and has wandered from the fold," repeating a phrase he had heard at Sunday-school the week before. And Mr. Ward

14

listened with anything but love of mankind in his heart, wondering whether he ought not to be included in the child's petition, esteemed church member though he might be in the eyes of those who did not see into his home life.

In the morning he faced a tired, listless, discouraged wife, sitting opposite him at a breakfast which had been prepared with his help, under protest, and with a spirit of nervous depression that from experience he knew well enough meant a miserable day at home.

He rose from the table with a really desperate feeling, saying again to himself, "It would be funny, if it were not so tragic."

"I'll try to find some one, Martha," he said feebly as he put on his hat.

"I don't much care whether you do or not," she answered indifferently.

He was tempted to grow angry, but checked himself.

"I'll advertise. I'm tired of sending to the agencies."

His wife did not answer.

"We'll do the best we can, Martha. There must be some competent girl in all this city somewhere."

"If there is, we never found one," Mrs. Ward answered sharply.

He wisely declined to discuss the question, and started to go out.

"I'll not be home to lunch," he said, putting his head in at the door.

There was no answer, and he slowly shut the door and started for his car at the next corner; and, of the many burdened, perplexed hearts carried into the city that morning, it is doubtful whether any out of all the number was more burdened than that of Mr. Richard Ward of the firm of Mead, Ward, and Company.

He sent in to three of the leading evening papers a carefully worded advertisement asking for a competent servant, and took up his days' work with its usual routine without the least expectation that any reply would come from his advertisements. It would, therefore, have given him a peculiar sense of interest in the future, if at about six o'clock that evening, as he went out of his office and with strange reluctance started for his home, he could have seen in a house not two blocks from his own a young woman eagerly reading the advertisement and talking to an older woman in a strangely subdued, but at the same time positive, manner concerning it.

❧ ❧ ❧ ❧ ❧ ❧ ❧ ❧

"Barbara, what you say is impossible! It is so strange that no one but yourself would ever have thought of it. You must give up any such plan."

The younger woman listened thoughtfully, holding a newspaper in her hand; and, as she looked up from it, the older woman had finished.

"At the same time, mother, will you tell me something better to do?"

"There are a thousand things. Anything except this."

"But what, mother? I have tried for everything. Our friends" (her lip curled a little as she said the word) "have all tried. No one seems to need me unless it is this family. Here seems to be a real need. It will be unselfish, mother, don't you think, to do something to fill a real demand, instead of always begging for a chance to make a living somewhere?"

She took up the paper and read the advertisement slowly.

"Wanted: A competent girl to do general housework. A good cook, able to take charge of the housekeeping for a family of five. American girl preferred. Good wages. Apply at once to Richard Ward, No. 36 Hamilton Street."

"I call it a good opening mother. And it's only two blocks from here. And I seem to fill all the requirements. I am 'competent.' I am a 'good cook.' I am an 'American girl.' And I am able to 'apply at once' because I have nothing else to do. So I do not see why I should not walk right over and secure the place before some one else gets it."

She rose from her seat, and the mother turned an appealing face towards her.

"Barbara! You shall do no such crazy thing. At least, you shall not with my consent. It is madness for you to throw yourself away! To think of my daughter becoming a 'hired girl!' Barbara, it is cruel of you even to suggest it. It is a part of your college foolishness. You have been jesting with me."

"No, mother dear, I have not." Barbara walked over to where her mother had been sitting, and kneeled down by her, putting her hands in her mother's hands, and looking affectionately up to her.

"No, mother, I am not jesting. I am very much in earnest. Look at me! Barbara Clark. Age, twenty-one, Graduate, Mt. Holyoke. Member of church and Christian Endeavor Society. Plenty of good health. No money. Educated for a teacher. No influence with the powers that be to secure a position. At home, dependent on and a burden to –" here Mrs. Clark put a hand on the speaker's mouth and Barbara gently removed the hand – "a burden to a good mother who has no means besides a small legacy, daily growing smaller, and the diminutive interest on an insurance fund that is badly invested in Western land. There's my biography up to date. Do you wonder that I want to be doing something to be making some money, even if it is only a little, to be a breadwinner, even if –"

"But to be a 'hired girl,' Barbara! Do you realize what it means? Why, it means social loss, it means dropping out of the circle of good society, it means daily drudgery of the hardest kind, it means going to the bottom of the ladder and always staying there! And you, Barbara, of all girls, fitted to teach, an exceptionally good student, bright and capable. Oh, how does it happen that girls who are your inferiors have secured good positions and you have not succeeded?"

" 'Pulls,' " said Barbara briefly.

Mrs. Clark looked troubled. "Is that college slang?"

"No, mother. Political. I mean that the other girls have had influence. If father were alive –"

"Ah, Barbara, if your father were living, there would be no talk of your going to work in a kitchen. And you shall not go, either. It is the height of absurdity to think of it."

"But, mother," Barbara began after a moment's silence, "do you realize the facts, the plain, homely facts of our existence? Every day you are drawing on Uncle Will's legacy, and next month's rent and grocery bill will eat a large hole in it. I have been a whole year at home, living in idleness, and eating my bread in bitterness because I could see the end coming. There is no one who is in any way bound to help us. Why should I let a false pride keep me from doing honest labor of the hand? And there is more to it than you imagine, mother dear. It takes more than a low order of intellect to manage the affairs of a family as a housekeeper, doesn't it?"

Mrs. Clark did not answer, and Barbara went on. "You know, mother, I made a special study in college of social economics. The application of those principles to a real, live problem had great fascination for me. Now, the hired-girl problem in this country is a real, live, social and economic problem. Why shall I not be able to do as much real service to society and the home life of America by entering service as a hired girl and studying it from the inside, as if I went into a schoolroom like other schoolma'ams, to teach? I love adventure. Why not try this? No one knows how much I might be able to do for humanity socially as a hired girl!"

Mrs. Clark looked at her daughter again with that questioning look of doubt which she often felt when Barbara spoke in a certain way. It was not the girl's habit to treat any subject flippantly. She was talking with great seriousness now, and yet there were ideas in what she said that her mother could not in the least understand.

"But even from a money point of view, mother, such a position as this is not to be despised. If my services are satisfactory, I can get $4.75 or even $5 a week, and my board and lodging and washing and incidentals thrown in. Suppose I had a position as a stenographer in one of the offices down-town. I could not possibly command over thirty dollars a month. Out of that take my board, lodging, washing, clothes, etc. And I could not possibly save out of it over ten dollars a month. Whereas, working out at service, I could save twice that much in actual wages. If I go into Bondman's store, for instance, as a salesclerk, I cannot get over five dollars a week, out of which I must board, lodge, and dress myself. Mother, I have thought it all out, and I feel that I must go in answer to this advertisement. I don't mind the social stigma. I do mind the bitterness of living in idleness at home. Let me do something useful if it is only for a little while. I am sure a servant can be useful."

"It is a dreadful thought to me, Barbara," said Mrs. Clark with a sigh. "I never dreamed that a child of mine would ever be a hired girl!"

"Say 'servant,' mother. 'Servant' is a noble word. Christ was a servant. Don't you remember Dr. Law's sermon on that word last Sunday?"

The girl spoke lightly, not knowing herself the depth of the truth she stated, and yet her mother started and shrunk back almost as if the words were sacrilege. It is possible, however, that the older woman caught some glimpse of that great Light in the social life of men; for, when she spoke again, it was with a yielding to Barbara's wish that was new to her.

"I don't understand you, Barbara. If only the money that your father saved for your education had been more wisely invested, we might – but it is too late to think of that now. It is the thought that you are throwing away your preparation for life on something beneath you that makes me oppose this. But, if you do go from this other motive, that changes matters somewhat."

"Of course it does, mother! Let me go. I should not be happy to go without your consent. I will do this: I will go for a trial. This is probably the only way I can go, anyhow. But, if after a reasonable time I find it is impossible for me to continue, if even my dream of any possible service to society turns out to be ridiculous or foolish, I will come back and – and – be a burden to you again, mother, until I find out what I am good for in this world."

"It is only on some such condition that I am at all willing to have you take this step, Barbara," said her mother reluctantly, as Barbara rose and stood up by her for a moment in silence. She suddenly stooped and kissed her mother, and then walked over to the window and looked at her watch.

"After six. I might as well go right over there now."

"They will ask you for references," the mother spoke up nervously, already doubting the wisdom of the whole affair.

Barbara resolutely gathered up her courage.

"I have Professor White's letter – the Chautauqua summer, mother, I can take those." Barbara referred to a summer's experience when in company with several seniors from the college she had served as a head waiter and housekeeper at a large hotel in a State Chautauqua Assembly.

"They are good as far as they go."

"Yes, mother, and I am sure they will go far enough in this case. This family –" Barbara picked up the paper and read the advertisement again to get the street number correctly – "is in crying need of help. They will not drive me away without a trial, references or no references."

Mrs. Clark did not reply, but looked and felt very anxious.

It was a serious step in her daughter's life and under any circumstances it might have a most serious effect on her future.

"This will leave me alone here, Barbara," she said as Barbara put on her hat.

"I think I can arrange to come home evenings," said Barbara thoughtfully. "We will settle it all right somehow, mother," she added with a cheerful courage she did not altogether possess. For since her mother's consent she had begun to realize a little more deeply what she was about to do.

"I hope so, dear," was the mother's answer, and then quite naturally she began to cry silently.

Barbara went up to her at once, and said, "Dear mother, believe it is all going to be for the best. I must be a breadwinner. Give me your blessing as if I were a knight of the olden time going out to fight a dragon."

"Bless you, dear girl," said Mrs. Clark, smiling through her tears, and Barbara kissed her silently, and then quickly walked out of the room as if afraid of changing her resolution.

Barbara Clark was not an extraordinary girl in the least. She was a girl with a quick, bright mind, positive in her convictions, with impulses that were generous and sympathetic, with very little self esteem, affectionate towards her friends and ambitious to do and be something. It seemed very strange to her that out of all her class in college she was one of half a dozen who had not been able to secure a position even of a secondary character in any school. Her father's death had left her and her mother alone in the world except for a few distant relatives in the West. Influences that might have secured a place for her were not used owing to a compulsory change of residence to another city caused by Mr. Clark's business failures. The intimate circle of close friends that had surrounded the Clarks during prosperity was changed for the cold wideness of a strange city lacking in personal friendliness. And Barbara and her mother had passed several weeks in Crawford, practically unknown, and with the growing consciousness that the little legacy and the insurance money were being drained seriously without hope of replenishing from any source so far as Barbara was concerned.

The girl's longing to be a breadwinner had driven her into many difficult places. Under some conditions she would have gone at once into one of the great mercantile houses of Crawford as one of its great army of saleswomen. But at that time of the year every position was filled, except a few places that did not offer anything but starvation wages under conditions that Mrs. Clark positively would not allow Barbara to accept so long as there was the slightest hope of the girl finding an opportunity to teach. So for several weeks Barbara had been, as she said, not unkindly, eating her bread at home in bitterness, because no one seemed to need her in the great world, where the struggle for existence seemed to her to be a struggle that made any other existence more and more impossible.

It was therefore not without a positive feeling of relief that Barbara Clark now hurried on to No. 36 Hamilton Street to secure the position of "hired girl" in a family of five, entire strangers to her; and she smiled a little to herself at the thought of her anxiety lest a number of other girls should have been before her and secured the place.

"I am in a hurry to look into the jaws of my dragon," she said as she turned the corner into Hamilton Street. "I do hope he will not swallow me down at one mouthful before I have had a blow at him with my – my – broomstick," she added, not caring whether the metaphor were exact or not.

She paused a moment when she reached No. 36, and was pleased to note that the house was not too large nor too small.

"Just an average family, I hope. Well, here goes," she said under her breath as she rang the bell. She had studied Latin and Greek at Mt. Holyoke, but "Here goes" was all she could think of to express her courage at that moment. After all, "Here goes" may be as good a battle-cry as any other to alarm a dragon, especially if back of the short cry is a silent prayer for strength, such as Barbara offered up at that moment.

There was no immediate answer to her ring and she rang again. Then there was the patter of a child's step in the hall and the door was opened.

"Is your mamma at home?" Barbara asked with a smile. The child did not answer at once, and Barbara took the liberty of stepping into the hall, still smiling at the child, who continued to look at her gravely. If dragons are to be met, why not with a smile?

"Will you please tell your mamma I would like to see her? Tell her I have come to see if she wants a –"

"A hired girl?" asked Carl suddenly, for it was he.

"Yes," continued Barbara, smiling; "tell her a hired girl wants to see her."

"All right," said Carl, slowly. He left Barbara standing awkwardly in the hall and started upstairs to call his mother. Near the top he met her coming down.

"Another one of those girls," began Carl in a good, sturdy voice; but his mother said, "Hush," and in a tired manner ordered him to go back upstairs and stay with Lewis until she came up.

She came down and met Barbara in the hall. There were two chairs there and Mrs. Ward sat down saying, "Won't you take a seat?" looking at Barbara closely as she did so.

"Thank you," said Barbara quietly. "I have come in answer to your advertisement in the evening news."

"Yes," said Mrs. Ward slowly. "Are you – do you think you can do our work?"

"I think so," replied Barbara modestly.

"Can you take charge and go on without being told how to do every little thing?" Mrs. Ward asked somewhat sharply. She was silently but rapidly noting everything about Barbara's face and dress and manner.

"Yes, ma'am, I think I can, after learning your ways."

"Your name?"

"Barbara Clark. I live with my mother on Randolph Street two blocks from here."

"You have worked out before?" Mrs. Ward was beginning to note the quiet refinement of the girl, and her first thought was a suspicion of Barbara.

"No, I have never worked out as a servant in a private family. I have been a waiter and cook and housekeeper one summer season at Lake View Chautauqua. The only references I have are from Professor White who had charge of the Assembly that year."

"Professor Carrol Burns White?"

"Yes, ma'am. Of Waldeau Academy."

"He was my son Arthur's teacher there. His reference would be enough." Mrs. Ward spoke eagerly, looking at Barbara even more keenly. "But you are not a – a – servant girl?"

"I am, if you decide to take me," replied Barbara calmly.

Mrs. Ward looked at the girl thoughtfully.

"I do not think – we – you are not of the class of servants I am used to. May I ask, is it – may I ask how you come to be seeking this work?"

"Certainly," replied Barbara cheerfully. "I have tried to secure other places, and have failed. I think I can suit you as a servant. I –"

Barbara hesitated. She thought if she tried to say anything about her studies in social economics, or the adventure of this plan as she had only vaguely dreamed it herself, she might not be understood. Better wait and let that develop naturally. So she stopped suddenly and sat looking at Mrs. Ward quietly.

Mrs. Ward hesitated also. It was an unusual situation. The girl had given enough evidence of being all right, especially if Professor White's recommendation was a good one. At the same time, there was a great risk in hiring a person of Barbara's evident education and refinement. How far would she want to become one of the family? What relations would have to be established between her and the mistress?

Bur Mrs. Ward was thoroughly tired out with a succession of disappointments in experiences with girls who were incompetent, ungrateful, and dishonest. The suggestion to her mind of a good, honest, capable woman in the kitchen and house who could relieve her of the pain of daily drudgery was a suggestion of such relief that she knew the moment that it came to her that her decision was almost made up to take Barbara even if the circumstances in the girl's life were strange and unusual. Barbara suddenly helped her to make the decision final.

"Of course, I am ready to be taken on trial. At the end of a week or a month if you are not satisfied, I shall expect you to say so, and that will end it."

"How much do you expect a week?" Mrs. Ward asked slowly.

Barbara colored. She had never been asked the question before.

"I don't know. Perhaps you cannot tell until you find out how much I am worth to you."

"Shall we say four dollars to begin with? We have paid more than that – but –"

"I will begin on that," replied Barbara quietly. "Now, of course, if I come, you will let me know exactly what my duties are, so that there may be no mistakes on my part."

Barbara had a good deal of shrewd business sense inherited from her father.

"Of course," replied Mrs. Ward almost sharply.

"About my staying in the house –" began Barbara. "I would much prefer to go home at night, to be with my mother."

"I don't think that can be managed." Mrs. Ward spoke with some irritation. "I shall need you in the evening very often."

"We can arrange that after I come." Barbara spoke gently again. "That is, if I am to come."

"Yes, – yes –" Mrs. Ward looked at Barbara very sharply, "Yes, you can come on trial, I am glad to get any one."

Barbara colored again, and the other woman saw it.

"Of course, I did not mean – I mean I am just about discouraged over my housekeeping, and I am nearly down sick over it."

"I am very sorry," replied Barbara gravely. Mrs. Ward looked at her doubtfully. It was one woman's sympathy for another spoken in four short words, but the older woman had had her faith in servants so rudely broken so many times that she could not at once accept the sympathy as real. She kept coldly silent as Barbara rose.

"Shall I come in the morning?" she asked.

"Yes, say nine o'clock."

"I will bring Professor White's letters then."

"Mamma," cried Carl, at that moment appearing at the head of the stairs. "Lewis wants to know if that hired girl is going to –"

There was a muffled cry from the bedroom upstairs as Carl suddenly disappeared, dragged back into the room by the older brother. Barbara smiled, and said, "Good night," and went out saying to herself as she went down the steps: "After all, the dragon was not so bad as I feared. I feel rather sorry for the dragon-keeper, Mrs. Ward herself," on whose character and probably behavior, together with that of her family, Barbara gravely dwelt as she walked home.

She grew quite animated as she told her mother the story of her adventures so far. The matter of staying with her mother evenings was a subject of earnest discussion. Both agreed that it must be managed if possible. Barbara went over the interview and gave her mother the best possible picture of Mrs. Ward.

"I am sure we shall get on very well. She is a tired-out woman, irritable because of her nerves. But I am sure she is a good woman, when she is well." Barbara concluded innocently. "The children will bother me, I have no doubt. But I know I can get on. I saw only one child. He has a rougish face, but not bad at all. Oh, the dragon is not what he's painted, mother."

"Not yet," said Mrs. Clark in prophecy.

"No, not yet," answered Barbara cheerfully. She felt almost light-hearted to think she had a position even if it was only that of a servant.

Yet she had herself said many times during her college course in the study of social economics that service was a noble thing. And, as she went up to her room that night after a long and tender conference with her mother, in which the two had grown nearer together than ever before, she seemed to call to mind the many passages of the New Testament which speak of Jesus not only as a household servant but even as a "bond-servant." And it came to her with heaven born courage that if the Son of God became "full grown" through his sufferings endured in ministering to others, why might it not be the way in which she and all other of God's children should develop their real lives and grow into power as kings and queens in the Kingdom? It is doubtful if ever before that evening Barbara had caught a real glimpse of the meaning of service. She did catch something of it now. She opened her New Testament, and it was not by chance that she turned to the passage in Luke, twenty-second chapter.

"And there was also a strife among them, which of them should be accounted the greatest. And he said unto them, The kings of the Gentiles exercise lordship over them; and they that exercise authority upon them are called benefactors. But ye shall not be so: but he that is greatest among you, let him be as the younger; and he that is chief, as he that doth serve. For whether is greater, he that sitteth at meat, or he that serveth? is not he that sitteth at meat? but I am among you as he that serveth. Ye are they which have continued with me in my temptations. And I appoint unto you a kingdom, as my Father hath appointed unto me; That ye may eat and drink at my table in my kingdom. . ." (Luke 22: 24 – 30)

Then she kneeled and prayed.

"Dear Lord, make me fit to serve. Use me to the glory of thy kingdom in the new life before me. Make me worthy to be a servant, to be like my Master. Amen."

So Barbara Clark began her new experience, which profoundly affected not only her own life for all time to come, but the lives of very many other souls in the world. And that night she slept the sleep which belongs to all the children of the kingdom, whose earthly peace is as the peace of God.

CHAPTER 2

It is Sweet to Toil.

IT was four weeks after Barbara Clark had been at work as a "hired girl" in the Ward family. She was sitting in her little room at the back of the house, writing a letter to one of her classmates in Mt. Holyoke. She wrote slowly, with many grave pauses and with an anxious look on her face.

"The fact is, Jessie," the letter went on after several pages describing a part of the four weeks' experience, "I have come to the conclusion that I am not born to be a reformer. It was all very well when we studied social economics to have our heroic ideals about putting certain theories into practice, but it is quite another thing to do it. I thought when I came here that I might do some great things; but there are no great things about it, just nothing but drudgery, and thankless drudgery at that. And yet Mrs. Ward – but I must not say any more about her. I have stayed out my month as I agreed to do, and tomorrow I am going to let her know that I cannot stay any longer. I think I shall try a place at Bondman's after all. It seems like a poor sort of position, after all the dreams we had at Mr. Holyoke; but anything is better than what I have been doing. I would not have mother know this, and I have not said as much to her yet. Poor mother! She must be disappointed in me. I am in myself. I am glad you are so well suited with your school. There is a good deal of the blues in this letter; and, to tell the truth, it is just as I feel. 'A Hired Girl for Four Weeks'! How would it read as title to a magazine article? I might get a few dollars for my experiences if I chose to exploit them. Instead of that, I have given them to you gratis. Shed a tear for me, Jessie, over the grave of my little, useless experiment in practical economics.

Your Classmate, BARBARA CLARK"

Barbara wearily folded the letter, put it in the envelope, directed it, stamped it; and then, being hardly more than a girl, and a very tired girl, and at the moment one disappointed with herself and all the world, she laid her head down on the little table and cried hard. To tell the truth, it was not the first time that the little table in the little room at the back of the house had seen Barbara's tears since she had come to work at Mrs. Richard Ward's as a "hired girl."

So this was the end of all her heroic enthusiasm for service. It had all turned out in disappointment. To begin with, the weather had been intensely hot all the time. The work was harder in many ways than Barbara had anticipated. Her mother had not been well. One week Mrs. Ward had gone to bed with a succession of nervous headaches. And so on with ceaseless recurrence of the drudgery that grew more and more tiresome. At the end of the month Barbara had summed up everything and resolutely concluded to leave.

She had not yet gathered courage to tell Mrs. Ward. The woman had been very kind to her in many ways. But she was not well, and there were days when things had occurred that almost sickened Barbara when she recalled them. When she went downstairs the next morning after writing the letter to her former classmate, Barbara had fully made up her mind, not only to give notice of her intention to leave, but to give Mrs. Ward all her reasons why she could not work as a "hired girl" any longer.

About ten o'clock in the forenoon Mrs. Ward came into the kitchen for something; and Barbara, with a feeling that was almost fear, spoke to her as she was turning to go back into the dining-room.

"I ought to tell you, Mrs. Ward, that I have decided to leave you. My month is up today, and I —"

Mrs. Ward looked at her in amazement.

28

"What! You are going to leave? Why, we are more than satisfied with you!"

"But I am not with you or the place!" replied Barbara so spiritedly that it was the nearest to an exhibition of anger that Mrs. Ward had ever seen in her, during the whole month.

Mrs. Ward sunk down in a chair, and a look of despair came over her face as she looked at Barbara. Barbara with a white face and trembling hands went on with her work at the table. She was preparing some dish for baking.

"Why – what – haven't we been kind to you? Haven't the wages – Mr. Ward was saying to me this morning that we ought to give you more. I am sure," Mrs. Ward continued eagerly, noting Barbara's set expression, "I am sure we would be glad to make it four and a half a week, or possibly five."

"It's not that," answered Barbara in a low voice. She took up the dish and put it in the oven, and then after a moment of hesitation she sat down and looked at Mrs. Ward gravely.

"What is it, then?" Mrs. Ward asked hopelessly.

"Do you want me to tell you all the reasons I have for leaving?" Barbara asked the question with a touch of the feeling she had already shown.

"Have you made out a list?" Mrs. Ward asked carelessly. It was that characteristic of the woman that had oftenest tried Barbara.

"Yes, I have," replied Barbara; and she added, with a different tone, as if she had suddenly put a check on her temper: "Mrs. Ward, I don't want to leave you without giving you good reasons. That would not be fair, either to you or to me."

"I ought to know," replied Mrs. Ward slowly. She still looked at Barbara sharply, and Barbara could not tell exactly what the woman was really thinking.

"Then, in the first place," began Barbara, "my room is the hottest room in the house. It is right over the kitchen, it has no good ventilation, and it is not attractive in any way as a room at the close of a hard day's work."

"It is the room my girls have always had." Mrs. Ward spoke quickly and angrily.

"Maybe that is one reason you have had so many," said Barbara grimly. The memory of the hot nights spent in the little back room framed Barbara's answer.

Mrs. Ward started to her feet. "This is impertinence," she said, while her cheeks grew red with anger.

"It is the truth! You asked me to give my reasons for leaving. That is one of them," replied Barbara calmly. "It is true of a good many other houses in Crawford, too. The smallest, least attractive, poorest room in the house is considered good enough for the girl. I know it isn't true of a great many houses that furnish as comfortable a room for the servant as for any other member of the family. But it is true of this house. I am not blaming you for it, but whoever made the house for the express purpose of planning to give the hired girl of the house that particular room, which in this case happens to be the hottest, most uncomfortable room in the building."

Mrs. Ward sat down, and again looked at Barbara keenly. Her anger vanished suddenly, and she said with a faint smile: "I don't know but you are right about that. Will you go on?"

"In the second place," Barbara went on slowly, "I have not had any regular hours of work. Four nights this week I worked until ten o'clock. Three nights last week I sat up until eleven with the children while you and Mr. Ward went to entertainments or were invited out to dinner."

"But what shall we do?" Mrs. Ward suddenly cried out despairingly. "Some one must stay with the children. And Mr. Ward and I have social duties we cannot neglect. I am sure we go out very little compared with other people."

"I can't answer your questions," Barbara replied. "But I know one reason why I feel like leaving is because I never know whether my work is going to end at eight or nine or ten or eleven o'clock. There are no regular hours of labor in a hired girl's life, in this house."

"Neither are there any regular hours of labor in a mother's life in a home," said Mrs. Ward quietly. "Is your burden harder than mine? Or is it any harder than your own will be if you ever have a home and children as I have?"

The sudden question smote Barbara like a new one, and in a moment she felt conscious of an unthought of problem in the social economics of housekeeping. She had not thought it all out, as she had told her mother. If the home life was never to be free from the necessary drudgery of life, why should she complain if in the course of service in a family exact hours and limits of service could not very well be determined? She was somewhat troubled in her mind to have the question thrust upon her just now. She was not prepared for it.

"In any case," she finally said reluctantly, "the hours are so long and so uncertain that –"

"But you have Thursday afternoon and nearly all of Sunday. You have more real leisure than I have."

"But you would not be willing to change places with me?" Barbara asked, looking at Mrs. Ward doubtfully.

"It is not a question of changing places. I simply want you to see that in the matter of time you are not abused. But go on with the other reasons." And Mrs. Ward folded her hands in her lap with a resigned air that made Barbara wince a little, for what she was going to say next would in all probability anger her.

"Another reason why I have decided to leave is the Sunday work. During the four Sundays I have been here you have invited in several friends to Sunday dinner. This makes Sunday morning my hardest day."

"It has happened so this last month, that is true," Mrs. Ward confessed reluctantly; "but it has been rather unusual. In three instances I remember the gentlemen invited were particular business friends of Mr. Ward, and he was anxious to please them, and invited them home with him from church rather than send them to a hotel. But such social courtesies are a part of a man's home life. What shall he do? Never invite a friend home to dinner for fear of giving the girl a little extra trouble?"

"I don't mind it during the week," Barbara replied thoughtfully, "but it does not seem to me to be just the thing on Sunday. A good many families make it a rule not to have extra Sunday dinners. Do you think it is quite fair?"

"We haven't time to discuss it. Go on," Mrs. Ward answered, not sharply, as Barbara thought she might. There were traces of tears in the older woman's eyes that disarmed Barbara at once. The excitement of her nervous tension was beginning to subside, and the attempt to narrate her grievances in their order was helping her to see them in their just light. Besides, Barbara had received some new ideas since she sat down to give her reasons for leaving. The next time she spoke it was with a feeling of doubt as to her position.

"There is another thing that I have felt a good deal, Mrs. Ward. You have asked me to give reasons. You will not think me rude if I go on?"

"I asked you to go on," Mrs. Ward replied, smiling feebly.

"Well, during the four weeks I have been in the family you have never invited me to come into the family worship, and you have never asked me to go to church with you, although I told you when I came that I was a member of a Christian Endeavor Society in Fairview before we moved to Crawford. I don't mind so much about being left out of the church services, but I cannot get over the feeling that as long as I am a hired servant I have no place, so far as my religious life is concerned, in the family where I serve."

Contrary to Barbara's expectation, Mrs. Ward did not reply at once; and, when she did, her voice was not angry. It was, rather, a sorrowful statement that gave Barbara reason to ask herself still other questions.

"There are some places in a family that are sacred to itself. Mr. Ward has always said that he thought the hour of family devotions was one of the occasions when a family had a right to be all by itself. Of course, if friends or strangers happen to be present in the home, they are invited into this inner circle, but not as a right, only as a privilege. We have had so many girls in the house who for one reason and another would not come into worship, even if asked, that for several years we have not asked them. But the main reason is Mr. Ward's. Is there to be no specially consecrated hour for the family in its religious life? Is it selfish to wish for one spot in the busy day sacred to the home circle alone?"

Barbara was silent. "I have not wished to intrude into your family life. I only felt hungry at times to be recognized as a religious being with the rest of you. Would my occasional presence have really destroyed the sacred nature of your family circle?"

"Oh, I don't know that it would," sighed Mrs. Ward. "I have only given you Mr. Ward's reason. He feels quite strongly about it. As to the church. Do you think I ought to invite my servant to go to church with me?"

"I would if you were working for me," replied Barbara boldly, for she was on sure ground now, to her own mind.

"Are you sure?"

"I know I would," Barbara replied, with conviction.

Mrs. Ward did not answer, but sat looking at Barbara thoughtfully. Barbara rose and looked into the oven, changed a damper, and then went over to the table and stood leaning against it.

"Your other reasons for leaving?" Mrs. Ward suddenly asked. As she asked it, Carl came into the kitchen and went up to Barbara.

"I want a pie. Make me a pie, Barbara, won't you?" he asked, climbing up into a chair at the end of the table and rubbing his hands in the flour still on the kneading-board.

Barbara smiled at him for they were good friends, and she had grown very fond of the child.

"Yes, if your mother thinks best and you will sit down there like a good boy and wait a little." Carl at once sat down, only begging that he might have the dish that Barbara had used to mix eggs and sugar in.

"I have told nearly all the reasons, I think," Barbra answered slowly and she turned toward Mrs. Ward. "Of course, there is always the reason of the social loss. I don't know any of the young women in Crawford; but, if I did, I do not think that any of those who have money or move in social circles would speak to me or recognize me for myself if they ever knew I was a servant."

Mrs. Ward did not answer. Barbara silently confronted her for a moment, and it was very still in the kitchen except for the beating of Carl's spoon on the inside of the cake-dish.

"And then, of course, I see no opportunity ever to be anything but a hired girl. How long would you want me to work for you, Mrs. Ward, as I have been doing for the last four weeks?"

"Indefinitely I suppose," answered Mrs. Ward frankly.

"Yes, you see how it is. If I should be willing to stay on with you, I might stay till I was an old broken-down woman, always washing dirty dishes, always messing in a kitchen, always being looked down upon as an inferior, always being only a part of the machine, my personality ignored and my development dwarfed, never receiving any more wages than when I began, or, at the most, only a little more, always in a dependent, servile position. Once a hired girl, always one so long as you choose to have me and I consented to say. Is that a cheerful prospect for a girl to consider as final?"

Mrs. Ward did not answer. Barbara had spoken out all that the four weeks had been piling up in her mind. Once spoken, it relived her; but she was troubled over the thought that, even if all she said were exactly true, there was still somewhere in the economic world a factor of service she had not fully nor fairly measured. She could not escape the self-accusation; "But ministry is still ministry. If this family really needs such work as I have been doing to help it work out its destiny in the world, why is not my service for it as truly divine as if ministered in other ways that the world so often thinks are more noble?"

Mrs. Ward still sat with folded hands and a strange look, as Barbara turned from her and began rolling out a small piece of pie-crust for Carl. When she had finished it and had put it in a platter, as she was turning with it toward the stove, she was amazed to see Mrs. Ward standing in front of her. She had risen suddenly, and had come over near Barbara.

"What you have said is too true, and a great deal of it, most of it; and yet, Barbara, if you only knew how much I need just such help as yours in my home, you would not leave me. Isn't there some way we can work it out together? I have not been to you what one woman ought to be to another. I have been nervous and faultfinding and – and – you have not said anything about that, I know, but, if you will stay, Barbara, we will try to study the thing out better, we will help one another. That is not exactly what I mean, but we will understand each other better after this talk, and perhaps we can be more just, and study how to better matters."

Barbara stood during this unexpected appeal trembling with a conflicting set of emotions. In the midst of all she could feel a return of something of the old feeling of heroism in service that had prompted her to answer the advertisement in the first place, and her pulses leaped up again at the thought of help from this woman to solve the servant question and work with her toward a common end. What could she do alone? Only four weeks of trial, and she had despaired of service. Already in the swift reaction from her despair, Mrs. Ward's words produced a great revulsion in her feelings. Surely all things were possible if both the woman of the house and the servant studied the question together. And her grievances! They were there still, and still real. But they were not without compensation if what Mrs. Ward said was going to mean a new start all around.

Still, as she faced Mrs. Ward with a troubled heart, she hesitated, going over again the trials of the four weeks, the hot, insufficient little room, the long and irregular hours, the separation from people, even from the very people in the house where she was serving, the daily drudgery, the hopelessness of any future – it all came up again to dash an enthusiasm that had apparently been killed out of her at the first attempt to turn practical things into heroic things. And let us say for Barbara what was a very true part of her true self; she had so great a revulsion of doing anything from impulse alone that a part of her hesitation now arose not from her doubts concerning Mrs. Ward's sincerity, but from her own fear of changing her mind, of seeming to act from pity for Mrs. Ward rather than from a genuine conviction that she had not been heroic enough to test her service long enough to prove something besides a few grievances. She was smitten even while Mrs. Ward was speaking, to think that she had not endured all the hardships of service to the limit of service.

"Of course, I don't know how we are going to arrange all the things that are wrong, but I have gone over all the ground you have emphasized his morning more times than perhaps you imagine," Mrs. Ward continued, and Barbara perhaps for the first time, gave Mrs. Ward credit for many thing she had hitherto denied her. "My wretched health, and cares and trouble with servants who have had no ambitions and no abilities such as you have, I think have all helped to make me seem indifferent and thoughtless. But I need you, Barbara. Really, I cannot bear the thought of being without help. You cannot realize what these last four weeks have meant to me in the burden lifted. You do not understand how capable you are in management. I ought to have let you know it. I am sure I have felt it deeper every day."

"You are flattering me now," said Barbara, smiling a little.

"No, only the truth as it ought to have been told you. My sickness, the children, my cares, Mr. Ward's business complications, some of which have been serious the last ten days, have all conspired to make me careless of you; but even my carelessness has been a sign of my confidence in you. Don't leave us now, Barbara. We need you more than you can realize."

What! Barbara Clark! Here has been trouble in this home, and trouble of a serious nature, and you have lived in your own troubles, absorbing all thought about yourself. She began to be ashamed. She turned towards Mrs. Ward.

"I don't want to seem to act on just my feelings alone. Let me go home tonight and think it out."

Mrs. Ward looked at her wistfully, and again tears came into the older woman's eyes.

"I am asking a great deal of you. Maybe I am promising a good deal for myself, too, if you decide to go on with us."

"You mean?" Barbara began, and then stopped.

"I mean that, if you will keep on as you have begun, I am willing to help make your place different in many ways from what it has been. I don't know all that this may mean to you. It is not an ordinary case, as you are not an ordinary servant girl. There is another thing I ought to say. If you remain with us, it ought to be a great source of satisfaction to you that the children think so much of you. Do you realize how much it may mean to a mother to know they are being helped in every way while with her servant? That is another great reason I don't want you to go, Barbara."

"Thank you, Mrs. Ward," Barbara answered, and the tears came into her eyes for the first time. Praise is sweet. Why don't we all give more of it where we know it will help, not hurt?

"We cannot spare you out of the home. We have not treated you right, but —"

"Don't say anything about that, Mrs. Ward," Barbara interrupted, a feeling of remorse growing in her at the thought of her "grievances." Some of them were beginning to seem small in comparison with her privileges. She was actually needed in this home. She was a real influence in it if what Mrs. Ward had just said about the children was true. Surely there was more in the position than physical drudgery. Could even a school-teacher expect to be more useful? A host of new questions rose in her mind.

"Let me go home tonight, Mrs. Ward, and I will return in the morning and give you my answer. In any case, I will not leave you, of course, until you have secured some one else."

"Very well, we will leave the matter that way," Mrs. Ward answered, and she went out of the kitchen as Carl began to clamor for his pie and Barbara turned to look at him.

But Barbara was strongly moved by this interview. It had begun with her heart full of discouragement and rebellion. It had ended with a feeling of doubt concerning her resolution to give up her position, with a renewal of her former enthusiasm. There were possibilities in the situation that she had not considered. And so, with all these new ideas crowding into her thoughts, she finished her work early that evening and went home.

Her mother met her with a happy smile, and instantly put into her hand a letter that had come in the afternoon mail. It had printed on it the address of a teacher's agency.

"Another polite note saying there are no vacancies at present, etc. Is that it, mother?"

"I opened it, Barbara. You remember you told me to if anything came from this agency, and I was going to send it over to the Wards' for you this evening if you had not come," Mrs. Clark said as Barbara took out the letter and began to read.

It was an offer from the principal of an academy in a neighboring State, of a fairly good position as teacher in the department of French and German, the two languages Barbara had made the most of at Mt. Holyoke.

"It's a good offer, Barbara. Just the position you can fill, isn't it?"

"Yes, mother," Barbara answered slowly. But she dropped the letter into her lap and sat thoughtfully quiet.

'What are you thinking of? Barbara, you don't mean to refuse, after all this waiting?"

Then Barbara told her mother all about the morning's talk with Mrs. Ward.

"I am in honor bound to stay with her, anyway, until she finds some one else. I promised. If I accept this offer, I must go at once, as the place requires an immediate answer in person. That would leave Mrs. Ward without any one just at a time when she is most in need of some one."

"She will let you off for such an unexpected offer as this, Barbara," Mrs. Clark spoke with eagerness. "You do not mean to lose it, to lose your chances of getting something better just for –"

"Mother, you must not tempt me," Barbara replied with a faint smile. And Mrs. Clark with a sigh made no further appeal. She knew from past experience that Barbara would not change her mind in such a matter.

After a long silence Barbara said: "Mother, I may decide to remain with Mrs. Ward for good. This morning I thought it was all a mistake and that I could not do anything. But since this talk with her I see some hopes of working out the problem. I really begin to think I may be of some use in that home."

"But you have not been happy there, dear. And I am sure the work is too hard for you. You are tired out."

"It is the heat, mother. I shall be all right when the cool weather comes this fall."

Mrs. Clark shook her head doubtfully; and, when Barbara went up to her room at last, her mother broke down and had a cry over the situation. Barbara had handed her the four weeks' wages, amounting to fourteen dollars. It was more than she could have saved on thirty-five dollars a month as a teacher, if she had been obliged to pay for her own board and lodgings and incidentals. But, in spite of all, Mrs. Clark could not understand the girl's evident purpose to go back to Mrs. Ward's permanently.

Up in her room that night Barbara turned to her New Testament with a purpose which had been formed since her talk in the morning. It had come to her mind, while Mrs. Ward was saying something about the need which she had of her, that there were a great many passages in the New Testament written especially for servants. And the idea occurred to her to search for all of them and make a study of them with special reference to her own case at what was now a crisis for her future. She would take one passage every week and dwell on it while at her work – if – she should decide to go back to the Ward's indefinitely.

She did not know where to look for all the passages referring to the slaves or bond-servants common to Christ's and Paul's times, but she was familiar with the beautiful verses in the second chapter of Philippians, and she turned to them reading from her Bible.

"Let this mind be in you, which was also in Christ Jesus: Who, being in the form of God, thought it not robbery to be equal with God: But made himself of no reputation, and took upon him the form of a servant (the Greek word is bond-servant), and was made in the likeness of men: And being found in fashion as a man, he humbled himself, and became obedient unto death, even the death of the cross. Wherefore God also hath highly exalted him, and given him a name which is above every name: That at the name of Jesus every knee should bow, of things in heaven, and things in earth, and things under the earth; And that every tongue should confess that Jesus Christ is Lord, to the glory of God the Father." (Philippians 2: 5 – 11.)

"The Son of God was a bond-servant." Barbara repeated the statement softly before she prayed. And never before had she prayed more earnestly for wisdom and humility and courage. Never had the girl felt a deeper longing to be of use in the world where she was most needed. "Help me, Son of God," was the burden of her prayer, "to decide now what I ought to do. Lead me in the right way."

In the morning she went down, and, meeting her mother, kissed her affectionately. Mrs. Clark looked at her anxiously.

"Yes, mother," Barbara answered gently, "I have decided to go back for good. I believe I can be of more use there than in a schoolroom. The dragon is very fierce and very tough, mother; and I have been scared and run away; but I am going back, and I want your blessing again. There are going to be some interesting fights with the dragon this time, mother, I am sure. For, if Mrs. Ward will do what she hinted at, the dragon will have two women after him instead of one. We will make it lively for him."

So Barbara walked over to the Wards', and, going right up to her room, put on her kitchen dress (her armor she called it), came down, and at the kitchen door met Mrs. Ward.

"I have come to stay," she said with a smile.

Mrs. Ward made a step towards her and Barbara thought at first the woman was going to kiss her. They both changed color, and then Barbara gravely said,

"I hope we may be able to do something together, as you suggested."

"I am ready to do something." Mrs. Ward spoke earnestly. "We cannot reform every thing at once, of course."

"Ourselves, for example," said Barbara quickly.

"To be sure," Mrs. Ward replied. Then she added with a show of emotion that had affected Barbara the day before; "I cannot tell you what a great relief it is to me to have you here. It means more to me than I can tell you just now."

"I am glad of it," Barbara answered simply, and at once began the day's work.

The next day was Saturday. In the afternoon, as Barbara was finishing the dinner dishes, Mrs. Ward came in.

"Will you go to church with me tomorrow?" She asked abruptly.

Barbara started, and then, recovering quickly, said, "Yes, if you really want me to."

"In the morning; we can arrange to get dinner when we return."

"What will this mean to you?" Barbara asked after a while.

"I don't know."

"Mr. Ward is willing?"

"Yes, I have talked it all over with him, and he is willing."

"I don't want to cause you needless embarrassment," Barbara began in a low voice.

"But it may not cause any embarrassment. We will try it, anyway."

"Do any other women in Crawford bring their servants to church with them?"

"Dr. Vane's wife always does. They are among the old families here. Very wealthy and –"

"I know Dr. Vane. He and my father went to school together in Fairview."

"Is that so? Then I will introduce you to them tomorrow."

Barbara could not avoid a smile at the thought. Nevertheless, she anticipated the event of going to church with Mrs. Ward with a degree of interest that she had not felt in her work as a servant since those eventful four weeks in her life had begun. A new factor had come into the problem. The woman of the house was going to co-operate with her. How far the co-operation was going to be carried, she could not foresee. Mrs. Ward's manner was both reassuring and at the same time uncertain, and Barbara could not tell how far she might go if matters became serious for her socially.

When Sunday morning came, Barbara joined the family at church time and they all started together. The church bells of Crawford were ringing, and in Barbara's heart there was a mingling of the peace of God with tumult, the peace that goes with the consciousness of human conflict over selfish human passion.

CHAPTER 3

Service is Royal.

THE WARD pew in the Marble Square Church was about halfway down the aisle and in the body of the house. As Barbara walked down the aisle, she was conscious of a feeling of excitement hardly warranted by the event. As she passed into the pew first, leading Carl after her as the arrangement of the seating had been planned by Mrs. Ward, she noticed Mrs. Ward's face. It was very grave, and there was again present in it that uncertain element which had set Barbara to guessing once or twice before how far her mistress would venture to co-operate with her in the matter of solving the questions belonging to housekeeping.

But Barbara was a young woman with a good reserve of common sense, and she at once dismissed all foolish speculations and resolutely gave her thoughts to the service of the hour. She was naturally and healthily religious and was prepared to enter into the worship with no other thought, except her need of communion and devotion and reception of truth.

When the minister came out of his study-room into the pulpit, Barbara noticed a look of surprise on several faces near her. She heard the lady in the pew next to her say in a whisper to another, "Where is Dr. Law today?"

"He is in Carlton. This must be Morton, their new minister."

"He looks very young. Do you suppose he can preach any?"

Barbara did not hear the answer, but she had not been able to avoid making a comment to herself on the youthful appearance of the minister. But, when he began the service by giving out the first hymn, the impression of extreme youthfulness disappeared. He had a good voice and a quiet, modest, reverent manner that Barbara liked. His prayer helped her. And, when he began to preach, there was a simplicity and earnestness about his delivery that was very attractive. He did not try to say too much. The sermon was written, but the reader had evidently tried to avoid being so closely confined to the pages as to lose a certain necessary sympathy with his hearers which the use of the eye alone can secure.

Barbara was really interested in the entire sermon, and as a whole it helped her. Her happily trained religious nature had taught her to look with dislike upon the common habit of criticism and comparison when attending a church service. The main object of going to church was to get help to be a better Christian, she had often said in little debates over such subjects while in college. If the sermon was learned and eloquent and interesting as well as helpful, so much the better. But, if it had every quality except helpfulness, it missed the mark. To be able to say after hearing a sermon, "That has helped me to be a better person this week," is really the same things as declaring that the sermon was a good sermon. Anything that helps life is great. All sermons that give courage or peace or joy, or inspire to greater love to God and neighbor, are great sermons.

So Barbara was lifted up by the message of the morning; and, when the service was closing, during the hush that succeeded the benediction, as the congregation remained seated for a moment, she uttered a prayer of thanksgiving and a prayer of petition for patience and wisdom in the life she had chosen, much blessed and comforted by the service of the morning.

As Barbara came out into the aisle again, Mrs. Ward was standing near the end of the pew opposite. She beckoned to Barbara.

"I want to introduce Miss Clark to you, Mrs. Vane."

An elderly woman with very keen blue eyes, and the sharpest look out of them that Barbara had ever seen, spoke to her abruptly but kindly as she came up, Carl still clinging to her.

"Very glad to see you, Miss Clark. You must come in and see us some afternoon or evening. Oh, I know who you are, just a servant; and we are rich, aristocratic folks and all that. My grandfather was a blacksmith in Connecticut. His ancestors were from Vanes of Arlie in Scotland. Good, honest working people as far as I can ascertain. I want you to meet Miss Barnes, who is helping us at present."

She introduced the young woman who was standing behind her, and Barbara somewhat shyly shook hands with a heavy-faced girl, who, however, smiled a little. Barbara was astonished as Mrs. Vane, and instantly concluded that she was a character in the Marble Square Church and in Crawford, as indeed she was.

"My father and Mr. Vane were in college together." Barbara said, as she moved down the aisle.

"Are you sure?" The sharp eyes seemed to look Barbara through.

"Yes, ma'am. I have heard father speak often of Thomas Vane. Before he mentioned the fact of your living in Crawford."

"Mr. Vane would be glad to see your father again. Ask him to call."

"Father died last winter," Barbara answered in a low voice. The tragedy of that business failure and sudden shock which resulted in her father's death was too recent to be spoken of without deep feeling.

"Dear me! It is strange Thomas never told me. Perhaps he did not hear of it. Is your mother living?"

"Yes." Barbara told her the street.

"She must come and see me after I have called. She is alone, you say?" And again the sharp eyes pierced Barbara.

They had reached the door, and Mrs. Vane tapped Mrs. Ward on the shoulder.

"Mrs. Ward, you see that Miss Clark comes to see me. I want a long talk with her. Don't be afraid, my dear. I don't want to know any more than you are willing to tell me. But I'm interested in you, and perhaps I can do something to help."

She hurried out, leaving Barbara in some uncertainty as to what kind of help was meant. Would this woman of wealth and social position help her in her plans for solving the servant-girl problem?

The Wards were still standing near the door, and Carl was pulling Barbara's dress and crying to her to hurry home for dinner, when the young minister came up and shook hands heartily with Mrs. Ward. At the close of the service he had come down from the pulpit and had gone through one of the side doors leading into the church vestibule. He had been talking with some of the people out there, but the minute Mr. Ward appeared he came over and greeted him.

"Very glad to see you and hear you, Morton, I'm sure," Mr. Ward was saying as Barbara came into the vestibule. "Been some time since you and Arthur came in to see us together."

"Yes, I've been too busy since I left the seminary, with the work in Carlton. How is Arthur?"

"Oh, he's quite well," Mrs. Ward answered as Morton looked at her. "We expected him home a month ago, but he had to give up coming at the last minute on account of some society doings. But –" by this time Carl had dragged Barbara out past Mrs. Ward – "allow me to introduce Miss Clark, who is –" Barbara looked at her quietly, and she continued, "who is working for us at present."

Mr. Morton bowed and shook hands with Barbara, saying as he did so, "I'm very glad to meet you, Miss Clark."

And Barbara, listening and looking with sensitiveness to detect a spirit either of patronizing or of indifference, could not detect either. He spoke and looked as any gentleman might have spoken and looked at any young woman who was his equal in society.

"Won't you come home to dinner with us, Morton?" said Mrs. Ward heartily.

"I'm stopping at the hotel; I think I had better not come to-day."

"Well, when do you go back to Carlton?"

"Tomorrow at two."

"Well, then come to lunch tomorrow noon."

"I shall be glad to, thank you," he said, and he bowed pleasantly to them all as he passed over to the other end of the vestibule to speak to some one else.

"Mr. Morton was a senior in college when Arthur entered," Mrs. Ward explained to Barbara as they walked out of the church. "He had opportunity to do Arthur a great kindness, and our boy never forgot it. He used to come home with him quite often during the last term Mr. Morton was at college before he

45

entered the seminary."

"He's a very promising young man," said Mr. Ward positively. "I like his preaching. It's sensible and straight."

"And interesting, too," Mrs. Ward added, her heart warming to the young man who had befriended her son. Just how much Ralph Morton had helped Arthur Ward not even the mother ever knew. But it was during a crisis in his young life, and the brave, simple nature of Morton had gone out to the young fellow in his trouble very much like a rescue. But men do not rear monuments to this sort of heroism.

Barbara walked on in silence, but in her heart she also had a feeling of gratitude for the young preacher whose courteous greeting no less than his helpful sermon had given her courage. At the same time, she was conscious of a little whisper in her mind which said: "Nevertheless, Barbara Clark, in the very nature of the case you are not privileged to move in the society of young men like Mr. Morton, as long as you are a servant. You may be college-bred, and you may be as refined and as intelligent as he is; but he could never look on you as an equal. His courtesy was paid to you as a minister would be courteous to any woman, but not as to an equal in any sense. You never could expect to sit down and talk together, you never could anticipate the enjoyment of his company or – or – expect that he would ever call to see you as – as he might call to see –"

Barbara colored deeply as she allowed the whisper to die away in uncompleted fragments of imagination. She was the last girl in the world to have foolish, romantic dreams of young men. She had never had a lover. No one had ever made her think of any such possibility. She was singularly free from any silly sentiment such as girls of her age sometimes allow to spoil the freshness and strength of a womanly heart. But she was romantic in many ways; and, being a woman and not an angel or a statue, she had thought at times of some brave, helpful, strong life that might become a part of hers. The world-old cry of the heart for companionship, the hunger, God-given to men and women, was not unknown to Barbara within the last year or two when she had begun to blossom into womanhood. The thought that her choice of a career in service had put her outside the pale of a common humanity's loving smote her with another pang as she walked along. It seemed that there were depths and heights to this servant-girl problem that she was constantly discovering, into which she might never descend, and out to which she might never climb.

Carl awoke her from her thoughts by dragging at her dress, and saying: "Come, Barbara, let's hurry. I'm hungry. Let's hurry now and get dinner."

Barbara looked at Mrs. Ward.

"Yes, go on with him if you want to. Lewis will be impatient. He ran on ahead before his father could stop him. I don't feel well enough to walk faster."

So Barbara hurried on with Carl and as she passed several groups of churchgoers she was conscious that she herself was the object of conversation. She could not hear very well, but caught fragments of sentences, some spoken before, some after, she had passed different people.

"A freak of Mrs. Ward's –" "Mrs. Vane's odd ideas –" "Perfectly absurd to try to equalize up –" "Girls have no rights to demand –" "Ought to know their places –" "No way to help solve the trouble," etc., were remarks by the different members of Marble Square Church that set Barbara's pulses beating and colored her cheek with anger.

"You hurt me, Barbara!" exclaimed Carl as Barbara unconsciously gripped his little hand tight.

"Oh dearie, I am sorry. I didn't mean to." In an instant she was calm again. What! Barbara Clark! You have not endured anything today! She had not anticipated anything before going to church. She had simply made up her mind to take what came and abide by it. What had actually happened was not a sample of what might happen Sunday after Sunday. Probably not. But it all went with the place she had chosen. Perhaps it was not at all the thing for Mrs. Ward to do. It might not accomplish any good. But then, it – she stopped thinking about it and went on to the house to prepare the lunch. When Mrs. Ward came in, she found Carl satisfied with a bowl of bread and milk and Barbara quietly busy getting lunch for the rest.

Mrs. Ward offered to help with the work; but Barbara saw that she was very tired, and insisted on her lying down.

"I'll have everything ready very soon," she said cheerfully; and, as she went back into the kitchen, she was humming one of the hymns sung in the service.

"What do you think about today?" Mr. Ward asked in a low voice as his wife lay down on a lounge in the dining-room.

"You mean Barbara's sitting with us?"

"Yes. Will it help matters any?"

"Oh, I don't know. I never would have done it if I hadn't happened to think of Mrs. Vane. She's rich and has an assured place in society. Her girls always come with her and she introduces them right and left to everybody."

"Yes, Martha, but Mrs. Vane is eccentric in all her ways. She is accepted because she is rich and independent. But have you noticed that these girls that come to church with her never get on any farther? No one knows them in spite of her introductions. I inquired of young Williams one Sunday if the Barnes girl was in the Endeavor Society of the church, and he said he believed she came three or four times and then stopped; and, when I asked him the reason, he said she did not feel at home, the other girls were better educated or something like that."

"That's just it. You can't mix up different classes of people. If they were all like Barbara, now, and knew their places –"

But just then Barbara appeared, and Mrs. Ward abruptly stopped. When Barbara went out again, she said, "I don't know whether her going with us today did more harm or good."

"It did the girl good, I am sure," said Mr. Ward.

"Oh, well, I hope it did. But I'd give a good deal to know what Mrs. Rice and Mrs. Wilson and Mrs. Burns thought about it. They knew Barbara, for they have seen her here several times at our club committee meetings."

"You don't suppose they would talk about it do you?" asked Mr. Ward sarcastically.

"They were talking about it all the way home, or I'm very much mistaken."

"What an inspiring thing it would be to a minister if he could only hear the conversation of his congregation for half an hour after church service is over," said Mr. Ward half to himself and half to his wife. "Whatever else he got out of it, he ought to get material for another sermon, at least."

"For more than one," added Mrs. Ward wearily. And then Barbara called them and they sat down to lunch.

But just what Mrs. Ward's three friends did say is of interest, because it is a fair sample of what other good people in Marble Square Church said on the way home, and the young preacher might possibly have thought that there is still a distinct place left for preaching in churches, if he could have heard what these three women had to say about Barbara.

They came out of the church, and walked along together.

"It was a good sermon," Mrs. Rice began. Mrs. Rice was a plump, motherly-looking woman and a great worker in the church and clubs of Crawford.

"Mr. Morton is a young man. He has a good deal to learn," said Mrs. Wilson positively.

"Dr. Law exchanges a good deal too much, I think," was Mrs. Burns' comment. "This is the third exchange since – since – last March."

"Mrs. Vane has a convert. Did you see Mrs. Ward's girl in the pew with her?" Mrs. Wilson asked eagerly.

"Yes. Rather a neat, pretty girl, and seemed to know her place. Mrs. Ward told me the other day that she is well educated and –"

"It is no sort of use trying to do that sort of thing!" Mrs. Rice interrupted, with energy. "I tried that plan once in Whiteville, and it did no good at all. Servants as a class cannot be treated that way. They always take advantage of it."

"That's what I have always said," added Mrs. Burns. "Look at Mrs. Vane's girls. She changes as often as any of us, and has as much trouble. The girls don't want to be treated like that."

"And, if they do, it makes no difference with their real position. No one will really ask them into society; and, if they did, they would not know how to behave," Mrs. Wilson exclaimed.

"It does seem a pity, though," Mrs. Rice went on, "that girls like this one shouldn't be allowed to have a chance like other people. What is she with Mrs. Ward for if she is educated and all that?"

"Oh, she has some idea of helping solve the servant-girl problem," Mrs. Burns replied. "At least, Mrs. Ward told me something of that sort. She does not know all about the girl herself."

"It's an odd way to solve the question – to go out as a servant herself," said Mrs. Wilson, and the other two women said, "That's so!" Yet all three of these women had been brought up on the theology of the orthodox teaching of the atonement.

"Did you see Mr. Morton speaking to the Wards? He was just as polite to the girl as he was to any one in the church."

"Of course; why not?" Ms. Rice asked with a superior air. "But now imagine Mr. Morton or any other gentleman in Crawford really considering a servant as they consider other people, even the factory girls or the clerks at Bondman's."

"Oh well, of course, there is a difference."

"Of course," the other two women assented. "But, after all, what constitutes the exact difference between honest labor of the hands in a factory or a store and in a home? If they are both service that humanity needs for its comfort or its progress, ought they not both to be judged by the standard of service, not by the standard of place where the service is rendered?"

"I think Mrs. Ward will find out her mistake, and be ready to say so in a little while. If she is going to bring her girl to church with her, I don't see where she can stop short of taking her with her everywhere else; and of course society will not tolerate that," Mrs. Rice said after a pause.

"Of course not. The whole thing is absurd. The girls must keep their places. All such eccentric women like Mrs. Vane do more harm than good," Mrs. Burns declared with decision.

"I had given Mrs. Ward credit for more sense," Mrs. Wilson said gravely. "But I must turn down here. Good-by."

"Good-by. Don't forget the committee meeting at my house tomorrow," cried Mrs. Rice, and very soon she parted from Mrs. Wilson, reminding her, as they separated, of the church-committee meeting later in the week.

The next morning after Mr. Ward had gone down to his business, Mrs. Ward said to Barbara: "You remember Mr. Morton is coming to lunch with us today. Would you like to sit at the table with us?"

The color rushed into Barbara's face, and she did not answer at once. Then she said slowly: "No, Mrs. Ward. I told you when I came, if you remember, that I never expected to sit with the family at meal-time. My place as a servant is to wait on the family then."

"Very well," replied Mrs. Ward quietly. "I simply asked because I want you to understand that I am ready to help you. Of course, you are not like the other girls who have worked for us. I have no doubt you could be perfectly at your ease with Mr. Morton or any one else in society." Mrs. Ward spoke with some womanly curiosity, for Barbara had not yet taken her into full confidence, and there was much in the girl's purpose and character that Mrs. Ward did not know.

"I suppose I could probably," Barbara answered demurely.

"Of course, you shut yourself out of society of people in your own rank of life by choosing to be a servant," Mrs. Ward went on abruptly. "You know that as well as I do."

"Yes," replied Barbara gravely.

"You know well enough that if I had introduced you yesterday to all the people in Marble Square Church, probably not one of them would ever have invited you to come and see them or even enter into any part of the church life."

"I suppose so," Barbara replied, flushing deeply. And then she said, "But I understand well enough that such conditions exist because in the majority of cases the girls who go out to service in Crawford would not care to be invited to the homes of the people in Marble Square Church, and would feel very miserable and ill at ease if they should be invited into any such homes."

"That is what I have often said. The servant girls are in a distinct class by themselves. They are the least educated, the most indifferent to refining influences, of all the laboring classes."

"At the same time," Barbara began; but Mrs. Ward was called out of the room by some demand of Lewis, who was still posing more or less as an invalid although he was able to be about; and Barbara went on with her work, conscious that the dragon was, if anything, bigger and fiercer in some directions every day.

About noon the bell rang, and Barbara with a little heightening color in her face went to the door.

51

Mr. Morton greeted her as she opened the door saying: "Happy to meet you again, Miss Clark. A little pleasanter and not so hot as last week."

Barbara returned his greeting by saying, "Yes, sir," and took his hat, while he walked immediately into the sitting-room like a familiar guest. Mrs. Ward heard him from upstairs, and came down at once, while Barbara went into the kitchen.

During the meal Barbara could not avoid hearing part of the conversation. She had always remembered what her mother had often said about servants telling everything heard in the family talk and she had tried since coming to the Wards' to train herself not to listen to what was being said, especially at the table when she was called in to stand and wait at the beginning or during the different courses.

But today in spite of herself she could not avoid hearing and knowing a part of the general conversation. She heard Mr. Ward good-naturedly asking Mr. Morton how long he expected to live in a hotel at Carlton.

"I'll warrant all the young ladies in Carlton have given him at least a barrel of slippers already," Mr. Ward said, looking at his wife.

"Will you give me the highest market price for all the slippers I possess so far?" Mr. Morton asked with a smile. Mr. Ward was in the wholesale boot and shoe business.

"I don't know. I don't think I want to load up so heavily on slippers."

"I assure you it would not ruin you," Mr. Morton answered lightly.

"I think with Mrs. Ward, though, that you ought to be getting a home of your own," Mr. Ward was saying when Barbara came in with dessert.

"My sister is coming up to Carlton to keep house for me if I stay there next year; I don't mind saying that the hotel is getting rather tiresome."

"If you stay? Why, are you thinking of leaving?"

"No, but I was hired for a year only."

"Listen to the modest young preacher!" began Mr. Ward with a smile. "Of course, Carlton will want you another year. If they don't, come down to the Marble Square Church. There is a possibility of Dr. Law's leaving before Christmas. He is growing old and his health has failed rapidly of late."

Mr. Morton said nothing in answer to this, and when Barbara came in next time they were all talking of the college days when Arthur and Morton were together.

Barbara had eaten her own dinner and was at work again, clearing off the dinner dishes, so that, when Mr. Morton rose in the other room to go, she heard him exchanging farewells with the Wards and promising to come down again before long. He went out into the hall, and after a pause Barbara heard him say: "I don't find my hat. Possibly Miss Clark hung it up somewhere."

There appeared to be a search going on for the missing hat, and Barbara's face turned very red as she took some dishes out into the kitchen and on turning to come back saw the missing hat on a chair at the end of the table, where she had absent-mindedly carried it on Mr. Morton's arrival.

She recovered herself in a moment, and, taking up the hat, brought it into the hall, saying as she confronted the minister: "I plead guilty to absent-mindedness, Mr. Morton. I carried your hat out into the kitchen."

They all had a good laugh at Barbara's expense, in which she joined and Mr. Morton removed the last of Barbara's confusion by speaking of his own absent-minded moments.

"The last time I had a lesson that ought to cure me," he said, smiling at Barbara frankly. "I left my sermon all neatly written on my desk in my room at the hotel, and brought with me into the pulpit several pages of blank foolscap paper that had been lying on the desk close by my sermon. I hadn't time to go or send back for the sermon, and was obliged to preach without notes except the few I could make at the time."

"Oh well, absent-mindedness is one of the marks of genius," Mr. Ward remarked, laughing.

"We will comfort ourselves with that hope, then, won't we Miss Clark? Good-by. Have enjoyed my visit very much."

Barbara went back to her work, blushing again over the little incident as she entered the kitchen, but grateful to the young man for the kindly, off-hand, but thoroughly gentlemanly manner in which he had treated it. It was a very little event, so little that it hardly seems worthy of mention, yet Barbara found her mind recurring to it several times during the day. During some baking in the afternoon, Carl was an interested spectator, and finally prevailed on Barbara to make him a gingerbread man. When she had cut it out and put some white dough on it for eyes, nose, mouth, and coat-buttons, she suddenly remarked aloud after Carl and herself had both been silent some time, "He is a perfect gentleman and that is more than can be said of some college-bred men."

"Is this a college-bred man, Barbara?" asked Carl the terrible. "I thought it was a gingerbread man. You said you would make me a gingerbread man. I don't want a college-bred man."

"This is a gingerbread man," replied Barbara hastily, as she turned to the oven and opened the door.

"Then who is the other man?" persisted Carl.

"Oh, never mind; I was thinking out loud."

"It isn't nice to do," remarked Carl reflectively.

"I don't think it is, either," Barbara admitted.

"Then what makes you do it?" insisted Carl.

"I won't any more when you are around," promised Barbara with much positiveness. The child seemed satisfied with this statement; but, when Barbara at last took the gingerbread man out of the oven, Carl suddenly said, "Let's give him a name, Barbara."

"All right," said Barbara pleasantly.

"You give a name," Carl suggested.

"Well, how about Carl?"

"No, I don't like that. Let's call him – let's call him Mr. Morton."

"Very well," replied Barbara hurriedly. "Run right along with it. Your mama is calling you, and I must finish my baking."

"Don't you think he looks like him?" Carl insisted as he grasped the figure by the feet, which in the process of baking had become ridiculously short and stubby, merging into the coat-tails.

"No, I don't think it's a striking resemblance," said Barbara, laughing.

"Well, I do. I think he looks just like him. I like Mr. Morton, don't you?" But at that moment Mrs. Ward called Carl in the tone he always obeyed, and Barbara did not have to answer him.

She finished her work in a serious mood, and in the evening in the little room over the kitchen she at first sat down to meditate as her custom sometimes was. But, suddenly changing her mind, she opened her Bible to seek out another of the passages that referred to the servant or to service, and after several unsuccessful attempts to locate a verse that she thought was in Thessalonians she found the passage in Ephesians sixth chapter, starting with the fifth verse.

"Servants, be obedient to them that are your masters according to the flesh, with fear and trembling, in singleness of your heart, as unto Christ. Not with eyeservice, as menpleasers; but as the servants of Christ, doing the will of God from the heart; With good will doing service, as to the Lord, and not to men: Knowing that whatsoever good thing any man doeth, the same shall he receive of the Lord, whether he be bond or free. And, ye masters, do the same things unto them, forbearing threatening: knowing that your Master also is in heaven; neither is there respect of persons with him."

"I wonder just what those words mean," Barbara thought. "'And ye, masters, do the same things unto them?' Of course, they could not change places as master and slave. It must mean a mutual honesty and justice and Christlikeness in their relations to one another." And then she gained great comfort from the last verse, 'neither is there respect of persons with Him.'

"My father in heaven," she prayed, "I have chosen my work, or Thou hast chosen it for me. Just what its crosses may be, I do not yet know. Whatever I shall be called upon to lose, Thou knowest. But in and through all, sustain me with this loving thought, there is no respect of persons with Thee, Thou who dost respect the service of men, and not their outward station. Sustain me by thy grace, in Christ's name, Amen."

When Thursday afternoon of that week came, Barbara remembered her promise to Mrs. Vane; and, when she went out, as it was her regular afternoon off, she told Mrs. Ward that she was going to call on Mrs. Vane.

"You will find her a very interesting woman. I don't know how much she can do to help your ideas. She is eccentric. But in any case you will find her interesting," Mrs. Ward ventured to say.

"I am sure she is," said Barbara.

"If she asks you to supper you needn't come back to get ours. I'll manage somehow." Mrs. Ward spoke kindly, and Barbara was on the point of thanking her and accepting the permission, when she noted Mrs. Ward's pale face and nervous manner. She had been suffering all the morning from one of her wretched headaches.

"Thank you," replied Barbara quietly. "But I prefer not to. I'll be back in time to get supper."

"Do just as you please," Mrs. Ward replied, but Barbara detected a look of relief on her tired face as she went out.

Mrs. Vane was at home and welcomed Barbara heartily.

"I'm all alone here, and you're just the person I want to see. Went to call on your mother yesterday. She is lonesome, and I've asked her to come and pay me a visit of a week or a month, just as she feels. I find that Thomas for some reason never heard of your father's death. Such things will happen even in a world of newspapers and telegraphs. I want you to tell me all about yourself and your plans. I don't believe you can do a thing, but I am ready to help you if you're the girl I think you are. The Vanes always were proud and aristocratic people; but, if we have ever stood up for one thing more than another, it was for honest labor in the house or the field or the shop or any where. I hate the aristocracy of doing nothing. All my boys learned a trade, and all my girls can cook just as well as they can play the piano, and some of 'em better. I'd rather eat their pie than hear their piano. Sit right there, dear, and be comfortable."

Barbara had not been in the house half an hour before she was deeply in love with the lady of it. After an hour had passed she was astonished at Mrs. Vane's knowledge of human nature and her grasp of the subject of servants and housekeeping problems generally.

"People will tell you, my dear, that I am an eccentric old lady with a good many crank notions about servants. The fact is, I try to treat them just as Christ taught us to do. That's the reason folks call me odd. People that try to do the Christlike thing in all relations of life have always been called odd, and always will be."

When Barbara finally went away after refusing an urgent invitation to remain to tea, she had made an arrangement with Mrs. Vane to meet with her and Mrs. Ward and a friend of both, to talk over some practical plan for getting the servants and the house-keepers together for a mutual conference.

"If anything is done," Mrs. Vane insisted, "it must be done with both parties talking it over in a spirit of Christian love. It never can be solved in any other way."

The date fixed for the conference was two weeks from that afternoon, and Barbara went back to her work quite enthusiastic over the future and very much in love with the woman who was known to most of the members of Marble Square Church as "that eccentric Mrs. Vane."

The two weeks had gone by quickly, and Thursday noon at dinner in the Ward house Barbara was surprised to find, when she came in to serve the first course, that Arthur Ward had unexpectedly arrived. He had spent two months of his summer vacation with college classmates on the lakes, and had returned sooner than his mother had expected, to stay until the term opened again.

"Arthur, this is Miss Clark, about whom I have written you," Mrs. Ward said a little awkwardly.

The young man looked at her with interest, and bowed politely. Barbara returned his bow simply, and did not speak. She felt a little annoyed as the meal proceeded and she was called in at different times. She thought the family was talking about her, and that the college student had been asking questions. Several times she was conscious that he was looking at her. It vexed her, although his look was always respectful.

The meal was almost over when Mr. Ward suddenly asked his wife: "Oh, have you heard, Martha, that Dr. Law had a stroke yesterday? Very sudden. It will result in his leaving Marble Square pulpit."

"No! How sudden: What will the church do?"

Mr. Ward was silent a moment. Barbara was just going out. She slackened her step almost unconsciously.

"I have no question they will call Morton."

"Will he come?"

"I think he will."

"Good!" said Arthur.

"Yes, Morton will be a success in Marble Square pulpit," Mr. Ward said positively.

Barbara went out, shutting the kitchen door. She did not hear Mr. Ward say, "If Morton goes on as he has begun, he will become one of the greatest preachers this country ever saw."

CHAPTER 4

To Be of Use in the World.

WHEN Barbara started that afternoon with Mrs. Ward for Mrs. Vane's to meet with her in the first conference, she had no plan of any kind worked out, even in the vaguest outline. She had told Mrs. Ward what Mrs. Vane had said before, and asked her whether she was willing to go with her. Mrs. Ward was very willing, and Barbara gave her credit for being as much interested as any woman might be expected to be in anything that was not even thought out far enough to be rightly called a "conference."

Mrs. Vane met them with her usual bright greeting, and again Barbara felt the sharpness of her look.

"I've asked Hilda to come in for a little while this afternoon. She doesn't want to stay very long, and I had rather hard work to persuade her to come at all. She's shy. Mrs. Ward, how's your headache? Or maybe this isn't your day for having one. I don't wonder your girls have trouble with you. You're so nervous with your headaches that I wouldn't venture to work for you short of ten dollars a week in advance. I wonder Miss Clark has stayed as long as she has."

All this the old lady said with astonishing rapidity and a frankness that amazed Barbara and made Mrs. Ward laugh.

"Miss Clark is learning to put up with me I think," Mrs. Ward said, with a kindly look at Barbara, who was pleased.

"Oh, I should think so," said Mrs. Vane, looking sharply from one to the other. "You don't either of you have many grievances, I imagine. Sit right there, Hilda!" she exclaimed as the girl Barbara had met on Sunday came into the room. "You remember Mrs. Ward and Miss Clark, Hilda? We met them last Sunday."

Hilda sat down awkwardly in the seat indicated by Mrs. Vane, and there was a moment of embarrassed silence. Hilda was dressed to go out, and Barbara could not help wondering how far the girl understood what the meeting was about. She began to feel a little angry at Mrs. Vane, without knowing just why, when that good woman very frankly cut across the lots of all preliminaries by saying: "Now then, Hilda, you know well enough what I asked you to come in for. We want to make a beginning of some sort at helping the girls who are out at service realize what their work means, and what they are worth to a family, and all that."

Hilda looked embarrassed, and said nothing. Barbara came to the rescue.

"Don't you think the first thing we need to do is to settle on some really simple plan by which we can reach all the girls and let them know what we propose to do?"

"You never can do it," Mrs. Ward spoke with some emphasis. "It has been tried before by Mrs. Rice and one or two others. The fact is, the girls do not care to meet together for any such purpose."

"Mrs. Ward is right and wrong both," Mrs. Vane said, with a nod to Barbara. "I'm not going to discourage you, but you have set out on as hard a task as ever a body undertook. The very people you want to help are the very ones who don't want you bothering around."

"Then perhaps we had better start with the house-keepers first," replied Barbara, feeling conscious of the bigness and badness of the dragon as never before. If you and Mrs. Ward and three or four more could –"

"But we have no plan," Mrs. Ward spoke up rather quickly. "You will simply find that the women of Crawford face the question without any ideas about it. We all agree that with rare exceptions the help we generally get is incompetent and unsatisfactory and not to be depended on for any length of time. And that's about all we're agreed upon."

Mrs. Vane looked sharply at Barbara and then at Hilda.

"Hilda," she said sharply, but at the same time not unkindly, "tell us what you think. What's the matter with all you girls? What's the reason you aren't all full-grown angels like us housekeepers?"

Barbara could not help smiling, although she had been sitting so far with a growing feeling of discouragement. As for Hilda, she had evidently been long enough with Mrs. Vane to be used to her odd ways, and was not disturbed by her eccentricities. She shuffled her feet uneasily on the carpet, and dug the point of a very bright red parasol into a corner of a rug.

"I don't know, Mrs. Vane," she finally said slowly. "I have no complaint to make."

"No, but I have. Now you know, Hilda, you didn't half do your work right this morning; and, if I hadn't come out into the kitchen, the pudding Mr. Vane likes would have been burned to a crisp. Wouldn't it?"

"Yes ma'am," Hilda answered, her face rivaling in color her parasol.

"And yet you had the clock there before you as plain as day. What were you thinking of?"

"I can't always be thinking of a pudding!" Hilda replied with more spirit than Barbara had yet seen in her.

"There, my child," Mrs. Vane said gently without a particle of impatience or ill nature, "I don't blame you much. I have let puddings burn, myself, when I was a bride beginning housekeeping for Mr. Vane. We must make allowances for human nature that can't always be thinking of puddings."

"At the same time," said Mrs. Ward with a trace of impatience in her tone, "somebody must think of puddings while they are baking. We can't be excusing human nature all the time for carelessness and lack of attention to the details of service. I think one great cause of all the trouble we meet in the whole problem is the lack of responsibility our servants take upon themselves. Out of a dozen girls that have been in my house within the last three years, not more than two or three could be trusted to wash my dishes properly. What can a woman do when after repeated instructions and admonitions her girls persist in using dirty dishwater and putting things away on the shelves only half wiped? We can't always be excusing them on account of

61

human nature. It may sound absurd, but I have gone to bed downright sick many a time because my girl would persist in putting dirty dishes back into the pantry." And poor Mrs. Ward heaved a sigh as she looked at Mrs. Vane, who sat straight and sharp-eyed before her.

"That's it!" she said sharply. "Responsibility! That's the word. But how to get responsibility into a class of people who have no common bond of sympathy or duty? No esprit de corps? The responsibility must grow out of a sense of dignity that belongs to the service. As long as the service is regarded by those who perform it as menial and degrading, the only thing we can expect is shiftlessness and all lack of responsibility."

"Responsibility generally goes with a sense of ownership," suggested Barbara. "But I don't see how anything like ownership can be grafted upon a servant girl's work. Now I wouldn't dare leave dishes dirty, because of my mother's training, no matter whose dishes they were. But I can easily see it is not very strange for a girl to slight any work in which she does not feel any ownership."

"There's another thing," Mrs. Vane said. "I've told Mrs. Ward so several times. She has always had a good deal of company and five in the family anyway a good deal of the time. She ought not to expect to get along with just one girl. At the close of a big supper it is almost half-past seven. The quickest girl can't wash up all the dishes properly in less than half an hour. If she wants to go out somewhere in the evening, what is more natural than for her to do the work in a hurry? She has been at work all day since half-past six. She works longer hours and for less pay than young men in stores get for clerk service that is not so important by half as the housework for a family. Now I'll warrant that Mr. Ward pays some of his clerks down-town three times what he pays the girl at home for almost twice the hours of labor. Wouldn't it be better and cheaper in the long run, Mrs. Ward, to hire two persons to do your work, at least for a part of the time? I'm inclined to think a good many of us expect too much of one girl. We work them too many hours. And we ought to remember that for most of the time the work really is what must be called drudgery."

"One girl in the house almost kills me. Two would complete the business, I am sure," said Mrs. Ward, smiling at Barbara. "Some of what you say is very true. But I am sure Mr. Ward would never think of giving as much for the work in the home as he gives for clerk work in the store."

"And why not, if the service performed is as severe, more than that, as important to your peace and comfort, and his own as well when he gets home? I know a good many farmers who think nothing of paying out several hundred dollars every year on improved machinery to lighten their own labor on the farm. But they think their wives are crazy if they ask for an improved washing-machine that costs twenty-five dollars or a few kitchen utensils of the latest style to save labor. That's one reason so many farmers' wives are crazy over in Crawford County Asylum. Men expect to pay a good price for competent service in their business. Why should they expect to get competent servants in the house for the price generally offered?"

"I don't think it's the price that keeps competent girls away from housework, Mrs. Vane," remarked Barbara. "I have figured it out that even on four dollars a week at Mrs. Ward's I can save more than I could possibly save if I worked for Bondman's at five or even six, paying out of that for board, lodging, and washing. If the price paid for competent servants was raised in Crawford to ten dollars a week, I doubt if the girls now in the stores and factories would leave their positions to enter house service."

"I believe they would, a good many of them, anyway;" Mrs. Vane replied with vigor. "You can get almost anything if you pay for it."

"But we must remember, Mrs. Vane, that the great majority of families in Crawford cannot afford to pay such prices for house-help. You have no idea how much trouble I am in for paying my girls four or four and a half a week. My neighbors who say they cannot afford that much tell me their girls become dissatisfied when they learn what we pay, and very often leave because I pay my girls more than other house-keepers."

"The whole question has as many sides to it as a ball!" exclaimed Mrs. Vane, rubbing her nose vigorously. "I think I shall finally go back to the old primitive way of doing my own work, living on two meals a day and washing the dishes once. You needn't stay any longer, Hilda, if you want to go."

Hilda, who had given signs of being in a hurry, rose and walked toward the door. Barbara also got up and, somewhat to Mrs. Vane's surprise, said: "I think I'll go too. I'll walk along down town with you, Hilda, if you don't mind."

Hilda nodded and Barbara was not quite sure that she was pleased to have her company; but Barbara had been thinking of a plan, and she needed to be with Hilda a little while in order to carry it out. So the two went away together.

They had walked down the street half a block, when in answer to a question Hilda said she was planning to do some shopping.

"Let me go, too; are you willing?"

"I don't mind," said Hilda, but with a note of hesitation that Barbara could not help remarking.

They went into several of the smaller stores, where both of them purchased one or two small articles, and finally entered the great store of Bondman's.

Hilda knew one of the girls in the store, and as they stood by her counter she introduced Barbara. The girl behind the counter stared hard at Barbara, but returned the greeting civilly enough, and then began to giggle and whisper with Hilda. Hilda seemed nervous, and repeatedly looked at Barbara as if she were in the way; and Barbara, thinking the others might have some secrets, walked over to the opposite counter.

She had been there only a minute when a young man sauntered up to Hilda and the friend behind the counter, and all three began to talk together. He was not a bad-looking fellow, but Barbara quickly put him down as of that class of weak-headed youths who might be seen almost any Sunday evening walking down the main street of Crawford in company with one or more factory girls.

This time Barbara did not attempt to avoid watching Hilda. A floor-walker in the store, going by at the same time, glanced sharply at the young man; but he was apparently buying something. The floor-walker turned at the end of the counter, and came back; and this time he looked longer at the two girls, and finally beckoned to the one behind the counter. She turned very red, and came over to where he stood. He whispered something to her that made her turn pale and instantly she went back and completed the sale of some little articles that Hilda had bought, giving the floor-walker, as she did so, several hateful looks. Hilda and the young man continued to talk together while waiting for the change. When it came, he seemed to hesitate and finally looked over at Barbara. Hilda said something, and he answered and walked slowly out of the store.

Barbara came over, and Hilda picked up her purchases.

"Are you ready?"

"Yes," Hilda said shortly, and after a word from the girl behind the counter they went out.

They walked along for some distance and then Barbara ventured to say, "Why didn't you introduce me to your young gentleman friend?"

Hilda colored deeply as she answered slowly, "I didn't suppose you would care to know him."

"Why not?"

"Well, you're not really one of us," said Hilda, looking sideways at Barbara.

Barbara could not help smiling. "How not one of you?"

"Mrs. Vane told me you're not really working out."

"What am I doing, then?"

"I don't know," replied Hilda hopelessly, and then was silent. Barbara made her decision rapidly.

"But I'm working out just as much as you are, Hilda. What is the difference?"

"You're educated," said Hilda shortly.

"But that has nothing to do with the fact of my being a servant in Mrs. Ward's house. I want to be friends with you, Hilda. Aren't you willing?"

"I don't mind," Hilda answered in a tone that Barbara did not think very encouraging. They walked on a distance without speaking. Then Barbara became conscious that across the street, nearly opposite, the young man who had come into the store was walking, and Hilda knew it as well.

Barbara looked at the girl again and the look determined her next question, even at the risk of losing what little hold she might have on Hilda.

"I am going to turn down here to Mrs. Ward's," she said as they reached a corner and stopped. As they stopped, Barbara saw the young man linger and finally stop his course. "I hope you won't misunderstand me," Barbara continued, looking into Hilda's face with great frankness. "But does your young gentleman friend visit you frequently at Mrs. Vane's?"

Hilda turned red, and at first Barbara thought she was about to give an angry reply. Instead of that she began to laugh a little.

"Yes, he calls sometimes. He's in the packing-house on night force."

Barbara looked at Hilda earnestly a moment, then abruptly turned, saying "Good-by," as she left. She did not look back, but was as certain as if she had, that the young man had instantly crossed the street and joined Hilda.

"And what business is it of mine if he has?" Barbara vexed herself with the question as she walked along. "I am glad she said he called. Mrs. Vane must know it. What business is it of mine if the girl meets him this way? He probably has very little other time. Shall a girl out at service have no society, no company? Oh, the whole thing is of a miserable piece with the entire miserable condition of service. What is to prevent girls like Hilda throwing themselves away on young men like this one? And who is either to blame her or care one way or the other if she does? And what possible prospect is there for me or any one to change the present condition of things?"

Barbara walked slowly back to her work, depressed by the events of the afternoon. What indeed could she do, if, as Mrs. Vane said, the very people that needed to be helped into better ways of living did not care to be helped if, like Hilda, they saw no farther and cared no more for better things than the little episode of the store and the young man suggested.

She felt so helpless in view of future progress that when she went up to her room that evening she was in need of great comfort, and in her search for the passages having servants in mind she came upon that one in Titus, second chapter, starting with the ninth verse.

"Exhort servants to be obedient unto their own masters, and to please them well in all things; not answering again; Not purloining, but showing all good fidelity; that they may adorn the doctrine of God our Saviour in all things."

"I don't think there is any danger of my 'purloining,'" Barbara said, smiling a little. "Although I have sometimes been tempted to do a little 'gainsaying,' especially when Mrs. Ward has one of her severe headaches. I really believe I have tried to be 'well pleasing' and also establish a reputation for 'good fidelity.' But that is a wonderful end to the exhortation, "That they may adorn the doctrine of God our Saviour in all things." If a servant, a slave in Paul's time, could go on serving with that end in view, what shall I say of myself? Is my service of such a character that it adorns like a jewel that which in itself is a jewel to begin with, the doctrine of God our Saviour? This is a high standard for a hired girl, Barbara. If you live up to it, it will keep you busy."

She offered her prayer with great earnestness that she might have the leading of the Spirit of Light, and in her prayer she remembered Hilda, fearing she knew not what for the girl, realizing as she never before had realized the many dangers that face working girls in large cities, and realizing, too, that, if she accomplished any great things as she sometimes dreamed she might, it must be done by the aid of a power greater than her own, for never before had she felt her own human weakness so strongly.

For the next three weeks the days went by in an ordinary way for Barbara; but, when she had time to reflect on them, she acknowledged that they had contained important events for her. It is because we are not able to see the bearing of what occurs day by day upon entire program of life that very often we do not count each day's sum as a part of the sum total.

Barbara had been unusually confined to the housework. Mrs. Ward had been again subject to an attack of nervous headache, and the whole of the care had been thrown upon Barbara. Mrs. Ward had now learned to trust her implicitly. This did not mean that the sharpness of her manner under stress of her headaches had entirely disappeared; but Barbara had learned almost perfectly how to anticipate her wishes, and the girl's great love for Carl and his complete trust in her, together with Barbara's cheerful, competent handling of the entire kitchen, had all united to capture Mrs. Ward's affections. She was content, even in her enforced idleness, to lie still with her pain and indulge in a great feeling of thankfulness for such a treasure in the house.

She was talking of it one evening with her husband.

"Do you realize, Richard, what a prize we have in Barbara?"

"She is certainly a remarkable girl. The most competent servant we ever had in the house, isn't she?"

"Without any comparison. And I want you to build that room as soon as you can."

Mrs. Ward had mentioned the matter of the room over the kitchen, and he had agreed that it was not suitable for a girl like Barbara.

"Or any other girl, Richard," Mrs. Ward had said.

"Yes, I'll have a carpenter come right up and look over the house. We shall have to raise the roof over the kitchen."

"Why can't we at the same time enlarge the kitchen so that Barbara can have a corner of that carpeted off for her own when she does not want to run upstairs? I saw Mrs. Rice's kitchen the other day. It is unusually large. One end of it is neatly fitted up with a table for books or sewing material, several comfortable chairs, and pictures on the walls, – a very cozy, comfortable corner, where her girl can receive her company or sit down to read or rest."

"But Barbara never has any company, does she?" Mr. Ward asked, with a little amusement at the look his wife gave him. "She hasn't any beaus, as all our other girls have had."

"No," Mrs. Ward answered thoughtfully. "But –"

"Well, what?"

"If she had, we would ask her to invite them into the parlor. Of course, we can't expect a girl as attractive as Barbara is to go through life without attracting some one."

"Unless her place as a servant –" began Mr. Ward.

"But why should that make any difference?" Mrs. Ward asked, irritated at the suggestion. "Oh dear, don't suggest my losing Barbara. Whoever gets her for his wife will get a perfect housekeeper and a rare, sweet girl in every way; but we shall lose the best servant we ever had, and then our troubles begin again, Mr. Richard Ward."

Mr. Ward was silent awhile, and then he asked about Barbara's plans for solving the servant question.

"I don't think she's done anything lately. I know she hasn't. Mrs. Vane sent over the other day to inquire when she was coming to see her again. My illness has kept Barbara very close to the house lately."

If Barbara had heard this talk, it might have encouraged her to confide in Mrs. Ward about a matter which had begun to trouble her somewhat, and that matter was no less than the action of her own son Arthur Ward.

It was now nearing the end of the college vacation, and the young man would soon be starting back to college to enter on his senior year. During the weeks he had been at home he had spent a great deal of the time about the house. He was behind in two of his studies, and was working a little to make up.

One day Barbara while at work in the dining-room heard him wrestling with a German sentence in Faust. He seemed to be unable to render it into good English, and Barbara naturally began to translate it for him without looking at the book.

"Isn't this the meaning?" she said, and then gave a very good interpretation. Arthur listening as he lounged on the sofa, book in hand.

"Of course 'tis. That's just it! What a numskull I must be! Wish you'd translate the whole thing for me," the college youth ventured to hint.

"Thank you, no, sir! I have other work to do," Barbara had laughed.

But from that little incident she began to note little irritating attentions paid to her, at first insignificant, but the last few days before the young man departed for college they were unmistakable, and Barbara was annoyed and even angered. She was really much relieved when he had gone.

But that experience was not at all to be compared with a discovery she made as to Arthur's habits, and it was a matter of regret to her afterward that she did not inform Mrs. Ward of it. It was the fact that several times she felt certain the young man had been drinking. She had never known him to be intoxicated; but she was sure he had more than once been dangerously near it, and it was a matter of surprise to her that Mr. and Mrs. Ward seemed so indifferent to it.

"Oh dear!" Barbara sighed as she went the rounds of her daily task, carrying this added burden of knowledge. "Is there no family without its skeleton? Ought I to drag it out for their inspection, if they don't know of its existence? It hardly seems to be my business. And they must be blind not to have noticed as much as has been apparent even to a servant."

It was a week after Arthur's departure that Mr. Ward announced the news of Mr. Morton's acceptance of his call to Marble Square Church. It was in the evening after the supper work was all done; and Barbara, as her custom had been for several days during the remodeling of her room, was seated with the family in the dining-room, which was also the favorite living-room, helping Mrs. Ward on some sewing. Lewis and George were reading, and Carl was playing on the floor near Barbara.

"I have Morton's letter of acceptance, Martha. As chairman of the supply committee it came to me do-day. It is a good thing for Marble Square Church. The people had sense enough to call him without going through a long course of candidating."

"When is he coming?" Mrs. Ward asked.

"Two weeks from next Sunday. The church at Carlton released him under special conditions, because they could get a man at once to fill his place. We're fortunate to get a man like Morton. He has a future."

"Barbara made me a gingerbread man once; and we called it Mr. Morton, didn't we, Barbara?" Carl spoke up suddenly after an absorbed silence during which he was apparently not listening to a syllable that was being said.

"Where is Mr. Morton going to stay?" Mrs. Ward asked.

"I don't know yet. I wrote him that we would be delighted to take him in here, but we didn't have the room."

"And I told Barbara," Carl broke in as if nothing had been said since he spoke last, "that I thought the gingerbread man looked just like Mr. Morton, and she said she thought it didn't. I wish Mr. Morton would come here to live, don't you, Barbara? Wouldn't that be fine?"

Barbara did not answer, and Carl got up off the floor, and went over to her and pulled her work out of her hands.

"Carl! Carl! You mustn't do that!" his mother exclaimed.

"Say, Barbara, don't you?" Carl persisted.

"Don't ask so many questions," replied Barbara, almost sharply.

"I haven't asked many," Carl pouted; but he went back to his game on the floor, wondering in his childhood mind what made the usually gentle Barbara so cross.

"I think the Brays can take him in. I hope they can. It's so near by that we can have him with us often. We'll be right on his way to church and back," Mr. Ward remarked as he settled himself to the reading of the evening paper.

While her room was in process of reconstruction, Barbara had been going home to stay with her mother. Mrs. Clark was only partly reconciled to Barbara's choice of a career; and when, this particular night, after the news of Mr. Morton's coming, Barbara arrived quite early (having excused herself soon on the plea of being very tired), Mrs. Clark noted the signs of trouble in Barbara's face, and instantly questioned her about it.

"Your work is too hard, too confining, my dear. It is not at all the work for such a girl as you are, Barbara. It will kill you."

"No, mother, I don't think it will," Barbara replied bravely.

"But I don't see what good it is doing to any one. You are just slaving yourself to death like any ordinary servant. Your talents as a teacher are wasted. Your social position is gone. You have buried yourself in a kitchen. Of what use is it? You might be in the world like other people, with some opportunities to rise and make the most of yourself, whereas now you are shut out from all the ordinary social ambitions and accomplishments of other girls —"

"Mother, don't, please," cried Barbara, and then to her mother's surprise she suddenly broke down and began to cry softly.

"There! I told you so! You are all worn out!" said her mother, coming to her and putting a loving arm about her.

"No, mother, I am not very tired in body. I'm just a little bit discouraged tonight," Barbara declared; and after a few minutes' crying, with her head in her mother's lap, she began to talk cheerfully of her plans. She was going to see Mrs. Vane again. She thought she could in a little time get Hilda interested and add one or two more to the inner circle. They were very kind to her at the Wards'. It was very much like home there. They were making a new room for her, and enlarging her kitchen. Barbara spoke of this last with a playful reference to a laughing remark Mrs. Ward had made while talking of the enlargement of the kitchen, – "You can set apart this new corner for company, unless you will use the parlor when your beaus come to call." "I don't think I shall ever need it, mother; you are all the beau I want," added Barbara merrily.

Her mother shook her head. "What company can you ever have, Barbara? You have forfeited all expectation of it by putting yourself into your present position. You are so situated that neither your inferiors nor your equals can meet with you socially. There is an impassable gulf between you and the young people of your own degree of education and refinement."

"Not necessarily, mother," Barbara stoutly protested. Perhaps a little unconsciously she was trying to give herself some hope. "Any one for whom I might care as a friend in the social world would not be influenced by my position."

"They couldn't help it, much as they might not wish to. Mrs. Ward is powerless. Mrs. Vane with all her wealth and influence, is powerless to give you any real standing in society. Try it and see."

"I will," replied Barbara as a plan occurred to her. "But, mother, why should I be shut out of any society I might choose to enter, simply because I am doing good, honest, useful labor with my hands?"

"I do not think you ought to be shut out, of course. We have gone over the ground a hundred times. But your position does shut you out. It is not a question of ought, but it does."

"Any one I might care for would not regard my position," said Barbara stoutly.

"Nevertheless, Barbara, you know as well as any one that because you are a hired girl in Mrs. Ward's house you do not have the place in society that you would have if you taught school in Crawford. Why, even in the church it is clearly a fact that you cannot get the recognition that you would get if you were doing something else. Don't you yourself see that plainly enough?"

Barbara was silent. She was going over in memory the last few Sundays at Marble Square Church. Since that first Sunday when she had gone with Mrs. Ward she had been every week except one. She would have been a very stupid girl if she had not noticed the difference between her reception by different ladies in the church and that given other young women. A few women to whom Mrs. Ward had warmly introduced her had treated her in every respect like any one else, with neither a patronizing nor a hypocritical manner.

She had been invited into a Bible class by the superintendent of the Sunday-school, and had been welcomed without any notice taken of her position; but, as the weeks went by, she was simply ignored by the majority of people to whom Mrs. Ward had introduced her. One invitation from a warm-hearted member of the class she had accepted, to take tea at her house; but her reception by other young ladies who met her there was not such as to encourage her to go again.

As far as the church was concerned, she found herself simply passed by. There was no uncivil or coarse contempt of her. There was simply an ignoring of her as a part of the Marble Square congregation. For various reasons she had not yet gone to the Endeavor Society. It met on Sunday night before the preaching service, and so far she had reserved her Sunday nights as sacred to her mother, who did not feel able to go out.

"I acknowledge what you say about the church, mother. But I may be partly to blame for it myself. I don't think the best people in Marble Square Church think any less of me for working as a servant."

"Maybe not, and yet even the best people are almost unconsciously influenced by social habits and traditions. Why, even the minister is influenced by them. This new young man, Mr. – Mr. – what is his name?"

"Morton," said Barbara, coloring; but her mother did not notice, as her eyes were very poor at night.

"This Mr. Morton, according to Mrs. Vane, is a remarkably good and sensible and talented young man; but, if you were to join his church and become a worker there, you could not expect him to ignore the fact that you were a servant girl. He could not even forget that fact when he was speaking to you."

"I don't know why!" Barbara exclaimed almost sharply.

"I only used him as an illustration of any educated Christian gentleman anywhere," said Mrs. Clark, looking somewhat surprised at Barbara's exclamation.

"A Christian gentleman," replied Barbara in a low tone, "would not make any distinction between a servant girl and a school-teacher."

Mrs. Clark sighed. "It is useless for me to argue with you, Barbara. You will probably learn all the bitterness of your position by painful facts. All the theories of social equality are beautiful, but very few of them amount to anything in the real world of society."

"I don't care for society!" exclaimed Barbara. "That is, for society represented by wealth and fashion. But I don't believe any real Christian will ever make any cruel or false distinction between different kinds of labor."

"It isn't that altogether," Mrs. Clark wearily said, as if too tired to continue. "It's a difference in social instincts and social feelings that separates people. You will find it out from experience in time, I am afraid."

When Barbara went back to her work the next morning, it was with a resolution to do something that perhaps the talk with her mother had suggested. In the afternoon she asked Mrs. Ward for leave to go and see Mrs. Vane, and it was readily granted.

When she knocked at the door and Mrs. Vane heartily bade her enter, she was more excited than she had been in a long time.

"I want you to help me make a test, Mrs. Vane," Barbara said, as the old lady sat, confronting her and looking straight at her with those terrible eyes. Barbara, however, did not fear them. She understood the character of Mrs. Vane thoroughly.

"Tell me all about it, dear," said Mrs. Vane.

Barbara went on, calming her excitement, but not her interest. When she was through, Mrs. Vane said: "I am perfectly willing, my dear. But I think I know how it will all come out, beforehand."

"But I want to prove it for myself."

"Very well," Mrs. Vane replied, with the nearest approach to a sigh that Barbara had ever heard her utter, and Barbara finally departed to her work. If she had realized what results would follow the test Mrs. Vane was going to make for her, she could not have walked home so calmly.

CHAPTER 5

A True Servant is a Lord.

THE "test" that Barbara had proposed to Mrs. Vane was not anything very remarkable either as a test or as an experiment. Mrs. Vane was to invite several people to her house some evening and invite Barbara with the rest, presenting her to her guests and treating her in every way like all the others. The curiosity that Barbara felt was in reality something in the nature of a protest against a remark made by her mother that society would not accept, under any conditions, a servant into its circle, and that not even Mrs. Vane with all her wealth and eccentricity and social standing could really do anything to remove the barrier that other people would at once throw up against her.

No sooner had Barbara perceived that Mrs. Vane was perfectly willing to do what she asked, and indeed looked forward to it with a kind of peculiar zest, than she began to regret having asked her. Nothing would be gained by it one way or the other, she said to herself hesitatingly as she pondered over it. What if she should be welcomed for herself? That would prove nothing and help nothing. She would go to Mrs. Vane next day, and ask her to forgive a foolish impulse that had no good reason for existing; and that would be the end of it.

But before she had found an afternoon to go and see Mrs. Vane that energetic lady had invited her company, and it was too late. Barbara said to herself that she could refuse her own invitation and not go, but Mrs. Vane next day wrote a characteristic note urging Barbara not to disappoint her.

"You must not hesitate to come for fear of putting me in any awkward position, my dear. I am independent of any verdict of selfish society, and the few friends who do know and love me will treat you as if you were a member of my own family, and you may be surprised at some things yourself. For I have found after a much longer life than yours that there is still a good deal of human kindness yet, even among people of wealth and so-called fashion. On the whole, however, you will be doomed to meet with what you undoubtedly expect. Wealth and family connections and, above all, position are counted greatest in the kingdom of men. The time will come when the first shall be last and the last first; and, when that time comes, servant girls will be as good as duke's daughters and eat at the same banquets. You are not willing to wait until then; so come to my feast and prepare to be overlooked. But don't stay away for fear of hurting me. The only way you can hurt me is to misunderstand me. I don't mind that from my enemies. They don't know any better. But my friends ought to.

Your friend, MRS. VANE."

This letter put Barbara more or less at her ease; and, when the night of the gathering came, she went to it quite self-possessed and prepared for anything. The reality of it she was not prepared for in the least, and among all her experiences she counted this the most remarkable.

It was to be rather a large gathering; and, when Barbara arrived, the front rooms were quite well filled. Mrs. Vane introduced her to three or four ladies standing in the front hall. One of them was a young woman about Barbara's age, elegantly dressed and very distinguished-looking, even to Barbara. Her name was Miss Dillingham.

"My mother was a Dillingham," said Barbara simply, as an opening remark for conversation.

"Indeed! Your name is –"

"Miss Clark," said Barbara.

"Oh, yes, Miss Clark. What branch of Dillinghams, may I ask? The Vermont Dillinghams?"

"Yes. Mother's father was from Washington County."

"How interesting!" The young woman smiled in a very interesting manner at Barbara. "Then we must be related somewhere. Our family is from the same county. Is your father living here in Crawford?"

"Father died last year," said Barbara, returning the young woman's look of interest.

"It's a little strange I have not met you before," said Miss Dillingham. "You have been shut in on account of your father's death." She looked at Barbara's simple black silk dress, which was Barbara's one party dress, very plain, but in perfect taste in every way. "But I thought I knew all the Dillinghams of the Vermont branch. Mother will want to meet you."

"Is she here tonight?" asked Barbara.

"Yes. She's in the other room somewhere. Ah! There's the new minister of Marble Square Church, Mr. Morton!" Miss Dillingham exclaimed. "I didn't know that he had come yet. I think he is perfectly splendid. Have you ever heard him preach?"

"Yes, I heard him once," replied Barbara; and the next moment Mr. Morton had caught sight of them, and came out into the hall and greeted them.

"Good evening, Miss Clark. I'm very glad to meet you again. And you, Miss Dillingham," he said in his simple but hearty manner.

"You are good at remembering names," said Barbara, because she could not think of anything brilliant to say. "I've understood that one of the difficulties for ministers is the task of remembering so many people."

"Yes, I've heard Uncle James say," spoke up Miss Dillingham brightly – "Uncle James is rector of St. Mark's in Crawford," she nodded by way of explanation to Barbara, – "I've heard him say that he could remember names that began with certain letters, but that he was completely forgetful of others. It must be very nice to have a distinguished memory for people's names. It is such a pleasing flattery to the people who are addressed. Every one likes to be remembered. He takes it as a special compliment."

"I don't know that I can claim any special faculty in that direction," the young minister replied, smiling. "Your names come near the beginning of the alphabet, C and D. Perhaps that helps me. The farther one gets into the alphabet, the more intricate and difficult the matter becomes."

"It's a very disappointing explanation, Mr. Morton," said Miss Dillingham, laughing. "We hoped, at least I did, that it was something personal about ourselves that made you remember us."

"What, for example?" said Morton gravely.

"For example, our – our looks, or –" Miss Dillingham turned to Barbara. "What should you say, Miss Clark?"

"Or our occupations," suggested Barbara, coloring a little.

"But we've no occupations," said Miss Dillingham carelessly. "At least, I haven't any since finishing at Vassar. Mother wants me to study photography. What would you say, Mr. Morton?"

"I?" The young man seemed unprepared for an answer. "Oh, I should say you would take a very good picture."

"Now, that's certainly a compliment, isn't it, Miss Clark?" she exclaimed, laughing again. "And yet they told me you couldn't talk small talk, Mr. Morton."

"I was trying to retrieve my blunder about the memory of the names," said Mr. Morton laughing with them. "But, if you really want my opinion about the photography, I think it would be a good thing for you to learn it. I believe everyone ought to have an occupation of some kind."

"Even society young women?"

"Yes, even they," Morton answered with his characteristic gravity, which, however, was not at all gloomy or morose. Young women like Miss Dillingham liked it, and spoke of it as fascinating. The reason it was fascinating was that it revealed a genuine seriousness in life. Not morbid, but interesting.

"What would you have us do, then? What can society girls like Miss Clark and myself do?"

Miss Dillingham asked the question seriously, or thought she did.

"Really, I am not competent to determine your duty in the matter," the young man answered, looking earnestly at Barbara, although Miss Dillingham had asked the question. "Perhaps Miss Clark can answer better than I can."

"I don't call myself a society girl at all," said Barbara, looking straight into Miss Dillingham's face. "I have to work for my living."

"No? Do you?" the young woman asked eagerly. "It must be very interesting. Tell me what you do."

There was not a particle of vulgar curiosity in the tone or manner of the speaker, and Barbara did not feel at all embarrassed as she answered quietly: "I am a servant in Mrs. Ward's house. The 'hired girl,' some people call me."

Miss Dillingham had leaned eagerly toward Barbara in anticipation of her reply. When it came, she evidently did not quite understand it.

"The – the 'hired girl'?"

"Yes. I do the housework there. Everything from the marketing to the dish-washing. I assure you I have an occupation all day long."

"Miss Clark is a good cook," Mr. Morton spoke up as Miss Dillingham stared at Barbara. "I can speak from experience, for I have dined at the Wards'." He smiled frankly and in perfect ease at Barbara, and she was grateful to him.

"It must be very – very – hard, and – disagreeable work," Miss Dillingham stammered, still looking hard at Barbara.

"Some of it is," replied Barbara. "But some parts of housework are very interesting. It's not all drudgery," she added, looking bravely at Mr. Morton although she was talking to Miss Dillingham.

Just then some new guests came down the stairs, and the three were pushed into the sitting-room. Miss Dillingham took advantage of the movement to excuse herself, and left Barbara and Mr. Morton together for a few moments.

"Do you think Miss Dillingham was a little surprised at your occupation, Miss Clark?" Mr. Morton asked, looking at Barbara intently.

"I think so. Nearly every one is. Aren't you?" Barbara had not meant to be so blunt. The question was uttered before she was aware, and then she stood more confused than at any time during the evening.

"Yes, I am," he answered frankly. "Of course, you are educated and – refined – and could be – school-teacher – or – or a photographer," he added with a smile that somehow relieved both of them. "Instead of that you choose to be a house servant. I have often wondered why."

Barbara colored. How "often" had he wondered? But she looked up at him and then looked down again. His eyes were very large brown eyes, full of thought, and Barbara was a little afraid of them.

"I had to do something. There was no school for me, and the stores did not offer any opportunity for a living. I chose the work of a servant because it seemed to me I could at the same time make a living and do something for the girls who work out because I was one of them."

"And can you, do you think?" he asked with great interest. But just then, to his evident annoyance, one of those persons who believe in keeping people moving on such occasions broke in with, "Ah, Morton, so delighted to see you. A dozen people right here want to meet you. Mrs. Jones, Miss Wainright, Miss Wallace, – Mr. Morton."

Mr. Morton turned from Barbara with a parting look and smile that she thought she had a right to remember all the evening, and met the persons his friend had mentioned.

"Permit me to introduce Miss Clark." He presented Barbara to the company, and she said a few words in reply to a word about the evening or the weather volunteered by one of the ladies. Then they directed all their remarks to Mr. Morton; and, there being no men in the little group, gradually she found herself outside the talk; and, as the company crowded together more in the room, she was separated from the rest and found herself alone, with no one to talk to. Mrs. Vane was in the parlor, and Barbara awkwardly stood by herself until the pushing of people gradually moved her up to a table where she was glad to find some views to look at.

She was turning them over and thinking of what Mr. Morton had said, when Miss Dillingham came up again with an elderly lady dressed in great elegance like the younger woman.

"Mother wants to meet you, Miss Clark. She wants to talk over the Dillinghams."

Miss Dillingham introduced her mother, stood listening a few moments, and then went away. When Barbara saw her again, she was again talking animatedly with Mr. Morton. Once they looked over toward her, and Barbara was certain she was the subject of their talk. Evidently Miss Dillingham was making inquiries about her.

"My daughter has been telling me that your mother was a 'Dillingham'."

Barbara nodded.

"We feel proud of the Dillinghams," the old lady said emphatically. "It's an old family with a record. Your mother was related to the Washington County branch?"

Barbara told her, adding a little proudly, "Mother is first cousin to the Radcliffs." The minute she said it she wished she hadn't; it looked like an obvious attempt to gain a point socially. Mrs. Dillingham regarded Barbara with added respect.

"The Howard Radcliffs?"

"Yes. The governor is mother's nephew."

"Governor Radcliff?"

"Yes," Barbara answered.

She was vexed with herself now for mentioning the fact, and her vexation was increased by remembering another fact, that during all her father's financial reverses the Radcliffs had coldly refused to help, and had been to some extent responsible for her father's final losses. She could have bitten her tongue at the thought of her silly eagerness to let this old lady know that she was somebody.

Mrs. Dillingham was looking at her with the greatest possible respect. Evidently the first cousinship and the Howard Radcliff connection were connections of the highest importance.

"Your father is dead, Alice tells me. Then you are living with your mother?" She did not wait to give Barbara time to answer, but said: "You must come and see us. I shall be glad to call on your mother, if you will give me the address."

Barbara gave her the street and number, and then, looking straight into her face, said, "Did Miss Dillingham tell you anything else about me?" It had begun to dawn on Barbara that for reasons not quite clear the daughter had not told the mother that Barbara was a house servant.

"Why, no. Is there anything more?" Mrs. Dillingham asked in a tone she never used except to persons who were her social equals. "Are you related to royalty?"

"Yes, I don't know but I am," replied Barbara, flushing proudly, a sense of the divinity of service almost overwhelming her even before that gorgeous figure standing so distinctly for the world's fashion and wealth. "I am a servant."

"How? What is that?" Mrs. Dillingham was puzzled. She stared at Barbara.

"You asked if I was related to royalty. The Son of God was a servant. I am one of God's children in the faith. And I told your daughter that I am obliged to work out for a living. I am in Mrs. Ward's house."

"Oh!" Then Mrs. Dillingham was silent, and there was an embarrassing moment.

"Well –" began the old lady slowly – "I don't see that that fact makes you any less a Dillingham, or a Radcliff."

"She's bravely standing by her Dillinghams," Barbara said to herself, and she began to admire the old lady.

"I suppose not," she said aloud. "But I thought you ought to know. And then –"

"Then I could call on your mother or not, eh?" the old lady said sharply.

"Yes, and recall your invitation to me," added Barbara, smiling.

"Invitation?"

"Your invitation to call."

"I shall be glad to see you any time," said Mrs. Dillingham gravely.

"Still, you would a little rather I wouldn't?" Barbara asked quickly.

The old lady colored. "Of course, the situation is unusual. I don't know why you're working out. Girls do such odd things nowadays. Is it in order to try the real affection of some young man, and get a husband for your own sake?"

"I never thought of that," replied Barbara, laughing. "No," and she became grave again in a moment. "I have no great choice in the matter. I am working out because no other position offered at the time and we are poor. I have to do something for a living."

"If you do get a husband while you are a servant, he will probably be a brave and a good man. Now, my girl tells me she is never certain of any suitor, whether it is she or her money that is wanted." The old lady looked wistfully at Barbara, and then added: "I admire your pluck, my dear. It is a Dillingham trait. Don't forget this: Blood is thicker than water. I believe Alice would do what you're doing if she had to."

"Would she?" Barbara did not say it, but simply thought it, wonderingly, as she looked over at the splendidly dressed young woman still talking with so much earnestness with Mr. Morton. And as she looked she could not help a feeling of jealousy at the thought of this proud, handsome girl with her secure social position.

Mrs. Dillingham was moving away. Barbara suddenly reproached herself with a lack of courtesy.

"I want to thank you, Mrs. Dillingham. I appreciate your – your – treatment of me."

"You didn't expect it, eh? But Mrs. Vane and I are eccentrics. You won't find any others here. We exhaust the material. There's a good deal of nonsense about money and position. But family – that's another thing. Princes have had to cook. Look at King Alfred. And he made a bad job of it, too. I'm sure you do better than he did. Don't forget you're a Dillingham." And she left Barbara alone again.

In a few minutes Mrs. Vane found her.

"Are you enjoying it?" she asked.

"Yes, I've had an interesting time so far," Barbara answered truthfully.

"I just saw Mrs. Dillingham talking to you. What did she say?"

Barbara told her briefly.

"Umph! She's of good blood. We don't agree in theology, but I like her for her good sense in other things. But, as she says, there are not many others like us. Let me introduce Mr. Somers, and Miss Wilkes, and Mrs. Rowland. Excuse me. I must go to Mr. Morton. I can't let Miss Dillingham monopolize him all the evening."

The new group to which Barbara had been introduced regarded her variously. Mr. Somers remarked that it was a warm evening. Mrs. Rowland nodded and said nothing, and presently turned to speak to some one else. Miss Wilkes coldly stared at Barbara, and in answer to Barbara's remark about some feature of the gathering she said, "Yes," and, as a young man went by, she turned her back directly on Barbara and began chatting volubly to the young man. Barbara remembered at that instant that Miss Wilkes was one of the young women Mrs. Ward had introduced her to the last Sunday morning she was at church. The Wilkes family sat directly in front of the Wards.

There was no one left but Mr. Somers; and he was saying, as Barbara recovered from Miss Wilkes' direct snubbing: "Have you met that Miss Clark that Mrs. Vane has invited here to-night? They say she's a mighty interesting girl, and she works out, too. Some people think Mrs. Vane carries things too far to invite hired girls to her house. That's one of the things that makes it interesting to come here. You never know who's going to be here. Like a kind of a grab-bag, you know. Don't know whether you're going to grab a bag of peanuts or a blank. Lots of blanks in society, don't you think?"

"I don't know; I haven't been out very much," replied Barbara demurely. She looked at Mr. Somers with interest. He was a tall young man in a regular dress suit, and there was a look of good nature about him that Barbara rather liked.

"Well, I should like to meet that Miss Clark. She's probably more interesting than most of the society girls. Do you know her? Do you see her anywhere?"

"I'm Miss Clark," said Barbara, and at the sudden look of surprise on Mr. Somers' face she burst out laughing, and he finally joined her feebly.

"The joke is on me, of course. But I never heard your name. Why don't people speak up when they introduce folks on these occasions? It might save trouble occasionally. Do you recollect if I said anything in front of your face that I might have said behind your back?"

"You said I was an 'interesting girl,'" replied Barbara, still laughing at Mr. Somers, who mopped perspiration plentifully.

"Well, you are; at least, so far," said Mr. Somers, looking at Barbara doubtfully. He seemed embarrassed, as if he did not know just what to talk about; and Barbara, who was perfectly self-possessed, helped him out by asking him to tell her who different people were.

Mr. Somers, who evidently went out a great deal, eagerly took advantage of the opening to give Barbara several biographical sketches.

"That old lady over there is Mrs. Reed. She's the richest woman in Crawford. That young man leaning on the piano is Judge Wallace's son. He's good-looking and knows it. That little thin lady in the blue dress, talking with Mrs. Dillingham, is the most interesting person in the house, present company excepted. Her husband lost every cent she had in the topaz mines out in Arizona last year, and shot himself at the bottom of one of 'em. That's Morton, the new preacher in Marble Square. They say he can preach people out of the soundest sleep known to the oldest inhabitant in Crawford. He's gifted and not bad-looking. We are said to resemble each other. The person right behind you is Miss Cambridge."

"What were you saying about me, Mr. Somers?" inquired a very plain-looking girl very nicely dressed, turning suddenly around.

Mr. Somers was disconcerted, but only for a moment.

"I was going to say you were the handsomest girl in the house except Miss Dillingham," said Mr. Somers gravely. "Let me introduce Miss Clark, Miss Cambridge."

Miss Cambridge shook hands with Barbara, and said in a low tone, "Mrs. Vane has told me about you." She seemed to want to meet Barbara, and Mr. Somers turned away with a pleasant word of regret at the interruption; but Barbara could not avoid the impression that he was rather relieved than otherwise not to have to take her in to refreshments.

"Will you go with me?" Miss Cambridge asked, and Barbara gladly consented. The refreshment-room was filled except two seats. They went over to them, and it was not until they were seated that Barbara saw that Mr. Morton was next to her, with Miss Dillingham beside him.

"You are having a pleasant evening, I hope?" Mr. Morton found time to say while conversation languished a little.

"Yes," replied Barbara.

"I hope to know something sometime of the results of your effort to ennoble service," he said with earnestness. Barbara knew the great, kind, brown eyes were looking straight at her. She raised her own, and looked into his face. She wondered at her courage as she did so. For it took courage to do it.

"I don't think I shall do anything great," she said.

"I think you will," he replied quietly. "I have great faith in that kind of life."

There was no opportunity for anything more, but Barbara cherished the few words as if they were of the utmost importance.

After they came out of the refreshment-room something separated her from Miss Cambridge, who had not proved as much interested as Barbara had imagined she might be; and again she was left to herself. For the first time during the evening she began to notice that she was attracting considerable attention. Standing in a corner by the door of the conservatory, she could not help hearing some one say: "Mrs. Vane has no right to go such lengths. It is the last time I accept any of her invitations. The idea of inviting hired girls to gatherings like this! It is simply an insult to all the guests."

"But the girl seems well-behaved enough," said a male voice.

"Very pretty, too," said another.

"It may be, but it's no place for her. It's an unheard-of thing for Mrs. Vane to do. She's done some very odd things, but this is the worst."

"I don't know," spoke up a voice that Barbara recognized as belonging to Mr. Somers. "A well-behaved 'hired girl' is less objectionable than a drunken count. That's what we had at Newport last winter at the Lyndhursts'. But then, I suppose he 'knew his place' all right."

Barbara found an opening, and moved away. The rest of the evening she was conscious of being largely left alone. There was no coarse or vulgar objection to her; but very many of Mrs. Vane's guests showed their feelings in a way, several of them said afterwards, so that Mrs. Vane would know how far she had mistaken her own place in society.

As the guests began to leave, Barbara nervously went to Mrs. Vane to say good-night, and found Mr. Morton with the

Dillinghams just saying farewell at the door. Mr. Morton bowed gravely to Barbara as he said good-night to Mrs. Vane and went out, Miss Dillingham taking his arm as they passed down the steps.

"I am going to ride," Mrs. Dillingham said to Mrs. Vane, as she waited in the hall. "The carriage is just coming around. I told the young folks to go on. It is a beautiful evening for a walk."

Barbara walked back into the sitting-room, and sat down by the table of prints and turned them over silently. When the guests were all gone, Mrs. Vane came in.

"What! you here, Barbara? I thought you had gone."

"No, I wanted to talk with you a little while," said Barbara with effort.

"Why, I do believe you are almost crying," the old lady exclaimed, coming up to her quickly. "Have you had a trying evening? Tell me all about it."

Barbara told her, and added something more that made the sharp eyes soften and the abrupt manner change to one of great gentleness.

"Don't worry, dear. It will all come out right, I know. Just go right on with your work. I understand it perfectly. I'm old enough to be your grandmother, and I've seen some remarkable things happen. The Lord takes care of more things than we give Him credit for. We must trust Him when we are in all sorts of trouble. And yours isn't the worst, by any means. But it's too late for you to go home now. I'll send Wilson over to tell Mrs. Ward, if any one is up there, that you are to stay here tonight."

So Barbara remained with the great-hearted old soul that night, and in the morning she went back to her drudgery, sobered by the events of that eventful evening, and trembling a little because she had intrusted her secret even to one so old and so loving as Mrs. Vane. But on the whole it comforted her. Under other circumstances she would have told no one but her mother. But Mrs. Clark was nervous and irritable, she did not understand Barbara, and lived a daily protest against her choice of life-work. To learn now from Barbara that she had come to think a great deal of the brilliant young minister of the great Marble Square Church would have seemed to Mrs. Clark like another madness, and what Barbara needed at this crisis in her life was not reproaches or tears, but encouragement and good-hearted affection.

She was a girl who gave her own affection quickly. From the day she met Mrs. Vane she had understood her. It was the same with Mr. Morton. It is a mistake to suppose that the greatest feelings must develop slowly. The feeling that Barbara experienced was not long in point of time, but she herself was the best judge of its strength. It is probably that she was afraid of its development in so comparatively short a time, and one way she took to ascertain the truth was to talk to Mrs. Vane frankly about it. Some things the old lady gave her that evening out of her own experience reassured her as to her own heart. Barbara had been afraid that her apparently sudden giving up of her life as it faced this other life was wrong. There was a tremor in the thought of unseemly haste unworthy of so sacred an event.

But, as the days went by, she found it was not so. She did not know all, but the experience that had come to her lent strength to her resolve to prove herself worthy of the faith he had said he had in that kind of a life, and the life she had chosen. At the same time, she faced with a gravity that was making her older than her years, the fact that the very nature of her position would make it impossible for her ever to realize an answer to her own heart from his.

So it was with mingled feelings of ambition that Barbara took up the daily round again. The results of the evening so far as her own position was concerned were insignificant. Mrs. Dillingham kept her word, and called on Barbara's mother. She also sent a note to Barbara, inviting her to call; and a little later she even included her in a quiet afternoon tea at her house.

Barbara ought to have accepted these overtures, for they represented a good deal of courage on Mrs. Dillingham's part. Barbara regretted a little later that she had not gone. But she had at the time, after that one night at Mrs. Vane's, concluded that she had attempted a thing that was of no value. She would approach the matter from another side. She was trying to think it all out, and had many talks with Mrs. Ward and Mrs. Vane about it, when an event occurred that threatened to interrupt all her plans and prove a real and serious crisis in her life as a servant.

It must have been three weeks after that evening at Mrs. Vane's when Arthur came home from college for a few days. He had not been in the house an hour before Barbara was annoyed by his attentions. They were so marked that his mother noticed it. Barbara was intensely indignant, and Mrs. Ward was much disturbed over it. In the afternoon, Barbara could hear loud voices in the sitting-room; and in the midst of it all Carl came out into the kitchen, crying and trembling, and saying that his mother and Arthur were quarrelling. Barbara, knowing what it was all about, could not help feeling relieved when the voices ceased; and after a time Mrs. Ward came out and had a talk with Barbara, apologizing for Arthur and promising that there would be no recurrence of the matter.

Barbara listened in silence, and when Mrs. Ward was through she said, "Arthur never would have behaved as he did if he had not been drinking."

"Do you mean to say that Arthur drinks?" Mrs. Ward almost shrieked. The experiences of the morning had given her one of her headaches.

"He does. He drank when he was here last fall."

"I can't believe it possible. He has nervous headaches. He bathes his head in alcohol to relieve it. He has told me so many times," exclaimed Mrs. Ward indignantly.

"But I know he was drinking this morning, or he would never have behaved so. No gentleman would ever have spoken to me as he spoke, Mrs. Ward, if he hadn't been under the influence of liquor."

Mrs. Ward lost her temper. Afterwards in quiet thoughtfulness, Barbara knew that her nervous tension was responsible for what she did.

"It's not true! You are too much given to thinking of yourself. You are too good for your place."

"Then, if I'm too good for my place, perhaps I had better not stay in it," spoke up Barbara in a sudden passion. But she was not an angel nor perfect, only a girl, worn out, perhaps, with the constant toil; and, at any rate, she was sorry for it the minute she spoke.

"You can leave any time! The sooner, the better!" Mrs. Ward said.

"I'm sorry," Barbara began.

"You needn't say anything. The sooner you leave, the better. We have all been worried to death over you ever since you came!" exclaimed Mrs. Ward; and, bursting into a hysterical fit of weeping, she retired to the lounge in the sitting-room.

If Barbara had waited until the weeping was over, and then gone in and told Mrs. Ward she had decided not to leave until her week was out, Mrs. Ward would have apologized. But the quickest passion is roused by injustice; and Barbara, smarting under the lash of Mrs. Ward's nervous-headache tongue, went at once to her room, packed her things into her trunk, put on her hat, and turned to leave the house. Down in the kitchen she found Carl crying.

"Where are you going, Barbara? Don't go away. I'm frightened, everything is so strange," he cried, lifting his arms to her. She took him up in her lap and kissed him.

"Why, you're crying, too, Barbara. Everybody's crying. What for?"

"I'm going home, Carl. Your mamma thinks I had better go home."

"Are you coming back?"

"I don't know, dear," Barbara answered as she put the child down.

"Don't go, Barbara," the child cried as she went out of the door.

"Don't cry, dear Carl. Perhaps I'll come back again," Barbara turned and called out to the child, kissing her hand to him.

CHAPTER 6

A Kitchen is as Royal as a Parlor.

As Barbara walked away from the Wards' that afternoon, she fully thought that her social experiment was finally over, and that she might as well write "Finis" to the dismal attempt she had made to solve even a small part of such a complex problem. But before she had covered the short distance between the Wards' and her mother's, she experienced a feeling a remorse that she had given way so miserably to her passion in the interview between Mrs. Ward and herself. She even hesitated at the corner before she started down the street leading home, as if she had some serious intention of going back to ask Mrs. Ward to receive her again. But it was only a moment's pause, and then she went on and entered the house, where she soon told her mother the whole story. There were tears on Barbara's cheeks when she finished.

"I seem to be a total failure in every way, mother. I haven't even learned grace to control my tongue."

"Neither has Mrs. Ward, from what you say," replied her mother with more spirit than was usual for her. "It seems to me she is the one who is most to blame. In fact, Barbara, I don't see how you could have done differently. She compelled you to leave."

"Oh, I don't know about that, mother. If I had not got angry — but it is all over now, anyway. There is no use for me to try any more," and Barbara broke down completely, crying hard.

Her mother wisely let her have her cry out, and then said: "I can't help feeling glad it has all turned out as it has. You know I have never approved of your going out to service. You simply throw yourself away."

"I don't know," Barbara replied sadly. "Somehow I cannot help feeling, mother, that I have failed to do what I ought to do, and that the regret over it will stay with me all my life. I began with a high purpose to accomplish something, and I have failed utterly."

"You have at least tried your best."

"No, mother, I don't think I have. I ought to have expected just such things as those that happened today. But it's too late to do anything now," she added with a sigh. "The question is, What am I to do? I expect it means going into Bondman's until I can get a school."

Her mother tried to comfort her, but Barbara was more depressed over the situation than she had ever been in all her life. She had met her dragon, and had been completely routed. And she had even at one time thought contemptuously of the dragon! But, as she went up to her room that night, she felt with great humiliation that the dragon had won and she would never again have the courage to look him in the face.

The next day she sent over for her trunk; and, when the expressman brought it, he handed her a note that had been given him by Mrs. Ward.

Barbara opened it in some excitement, thinking it might be a request to come back. But it was a scrawl from Carl, who had at different times been encouraged by Barbara to print real letters to his father and brothers.

"Dear Barbara: I am very sorry you have gone. Won't you come back? I do not feel very well today. My head aches. If you will come back I will be good to you."
Your loving CARL."

When she had read this note, which Mrs. Ward had let Carl send, she sat down on her trunk and cried again. It seemed all so dismal a mistake, such a waste of her life so far. She did not look forward to the future with any degree of hopefulness. It seemed as if all her high ambitions were destroyed and all of her ideals swept out of her life.

The next two days she spent in helping her mother with some sewing and in little duties about the house. In every moment of leisure from these duties her thought at once went back to her ambition to serve, and the more she dwelt upon it, the more hopeless she grew.

It was the morning of the third day after she had left Mrs. Ward, and she was at work washing the breakfast dishes, when a note was brought to her. The reading of it stirred her pulses as she stood in the kitchen and read:

"My dear Barbara: Carl has been taken ill, and is a very sick child. He calls for you constantly. Can you come and see him? I do not dare ask if you will come to stay again, after my unkind words to you. But I am sure you will be willing to please Carl by coming to see him. The dear child is very ill indeed.
MRS. RICHARD WARD."

Barbara went out to the sitting-room at once, and showed the note to her mother.

"Of course, I will go right over there," Barbara said as she put on her hat.

"Will you stay if Mrs. Ward asks you to?" her mother asked with a tone which conveyed curiosity mingled with dissuasion.

"I don't know," Barbara hesitated. "I don't think she will ask me to come back."

"I think she will," replied Mrs. Clark. "And my advice, Barbara, is that you say no. I can't bear to think of you as finally becoming nothing but a servant."

Barbara did not answer. She said good-by to her mother and started for the Wards'. On her way her mother's last words smote her again and again.

"Nothing but a servant!"

Was it, then, so low a place for a human being to fill – a place of service where the help rendered was a necessity to a family? Was this place in society so insignificant or so contemptible that it could be characterized as "nothing" but a servant? What was worth while, then, in the world? Was it worth more to the world to paint pictures, or sell dry-goods, or teach school, or spend time in eating and drinking and dressing up for parties as so many rich and fashionable people in society did all the time? Were these things more useful than the work she had been doing, or caring for the physical needs of a home so that it could develop in the strongest and best ways?

Mrs. Ward met her at the door as she was about to ring the bell. She had evidently been looking for her out of the front window.

"I'm so glad you have come," she said, and in a few words she explained Carl's condition. She did not say a word about the scene between herself and Barbara, and Barbara did not introduce the subject.

"Carl was taken down with the fever night before last. He has been steadily growing worse. Will you go right up and see him now?"

Mrs. Ward led the way, and Barbara followed, feeling strangely depressed as if in anticipation of some great trouble. She sat down by Carl and the child knew her.

"Little man," she said, using a term she had often given him, "are you glad to see Barbara? I am sorry you are not well. So sorry."

"You come to stay?" asked Carl, speaking with difficulty.

"I'll stay with you awhile," Barbara answered, glancing at Mrs. Ward who was standing at the foot of the bed.

"I mean all the time, all the time," Carl repeated slowly.

"If your mother wants me to," replied Barbara, who in the passage from home to the Wards' had really made up her mind to stay if she was asked.

"Oh, I do want you to stay, Barbara!" cried Mrs. Ward suddenly. Then Barbara saw that she was worn out with the care of Carl for two nights and the housework in addition.

"Mr. Ward has not been able to get a nurse yet, and – and – we have not begun to – look around for – a girl – Carl's sudden illness –"

"I'll come back and help if you want me to," said Barbara quietly. All this time she had been holding Carl's hand. He clung to her with feverish strength.

"And we'll have good times in the kitchen. And will you make me another gingerbread man like Mr. Morton, same's the one we made before? You know. Barbara?"

"Yes, yes, little man, I will do anything for you. We'll have good times together again."

"And you'll stay always, won't you, Barbara, always?"

"I'm going to stay, dear. Don't talk any more now," Barbara said gently. And Carl seemed satisfied, dropping into a condition of stupor which the doctor who called an hour later regarded with grave attention.

While the doctor was attending to Carl and Mrs. Ward was anxiously standing by him, Barbara slipped down into the dining-room, and found matters in confusion as she had expected. The breakfast dishes were still on the table, the kitchen fire had gone out, and all the rooms downstairs were in disorder. She quickly set to work to restore order; and, when the doctor had gone and Mrs. Ward had come down, Barbara had cleaned up the dishes and the dining-room, and had begun to set the kitchen to rights.

Mrs. Ward stepping out into the kitchen; and, as Barbara was moving into the dining-room for something, she suddenly threw her arms about her, and cried: "You don't know what it means to me to have you back again. We have had three miserable days. Carl is a very sick child. I am all worn out!" She then sat down and cried nervously.

Barbara felt embarrassed at first in the role of comforter. But she was quick to see how dependent Mrs. Ward had become. It was, after all, as woman to woman that they were related now in their common anxiety for Carl. And Barbara tired to cheer the mother by every word of encouragement she could think of while she busied herself with the necessary details of the kitchen work.

In the afternoon she went over to her mother's, and told her what her decision was. Mrs. Clark sadly consented, and did not make so strong an objection as Barbara had feared. So the little trunk was carried again to the old room, and Barbara realized that her career had received a new beginning in some sense, she hardly knew how. One thing she felt very strongly, however, and that was that under the stress of need at the Wards' she was doing exactly the right thing in going back to her life of service there. Whatever the days might have for her of opportunity in the future for large service in the greater problem, it was to her mind very clear that her immediate duty lay within the circle of this one family that needed her.

She realized this more and more strongly as the next few days brought to her and the family a new and sad experience. As Carl's condition grew worse, she spent more and more of her time with him. Mrs. Ward secured a good nurse, but Carl cried in his delirium for Barbara, and she sat with him many hours of every day. She was with him when the end came which they had all come to know was inevitable. It will always be one of the comforting thoughts of Barbara's life that she won and held the love of this child. All that came to her long after. But, as this little life slowly breathed itself out in the early gray of that morning, with the weeping father and mother and the two boys as they gathered around the bed, she felt a tender sympathy for them all as if she, too, had been one of the members of the family. Carl had insisted to the very last on clinging to his mother and to Barbara. Each woman held a hand as the child's soul went out of the frail body to God who gave it.

Mr. Morton, who had been a frequent visitor at the house during the trouble that had come upon it, was sitting by Mr. Ward that morning. When the end finally came, he kneeled down by Mr. Ward's side, and Barbara was conscious that the minister's strong, right hand was laid in compassion on the bereaved father's hand as he prayed for consolation.

"Oh our Father," he cried, and his voice brought a relief even in that moment of sharp sorrow to the family, "mercifully reveal to us the happiness of the soul thou hast just caught up into Thy bosom. We know he is safe in Thy arms. Comfort us with the comfort which earth does not have to give; take us also into the embrace of a love which gave an only-begotten Son for a dying and mourning world. The God of comfort bless this household. In the name of Christ, Amen."

Two days later, after the funeral service, at which Mr. Morton was present as pastor and friend, Mrs. Ward broke down completely and went to bed, leaving the care of the house and the family upon Barbara. The girl bore up under the responsibility bravely. She was conscious of the fact that she was necessary to the comfort of a home. The bonds of her service rested lightly on her because she knew she was of use in the kingdom of God.

The relation between Mrs. Ward and Barbara during those days of grief became very close and affectionate. Through all the older woman's nervous and even irritable illness Barbara nursed and attended her with admirable patience, giving her the best possible care and trying to relieve her of every possible anxiety as to the affairs of the house itself.

"You have been like a daughter to me, Barbara," Mrs. Ward said to her one day three weeks after Carl's death. "I do not know what would have become of us if you had not come back." Barbara was arranging her pillows; and, as she stooped down over her, Mrs. Ward put an arm about Barbara's neck, drew her down, and kissed her. When Barbara raised her head, the tears shone on her face.

"Service has been very sweet to me, Mrs. Ward, since I returned. I have liked to believe that I have been needed."

"You have been a wonderful comfort to us. You are like one of the family since Carl's leaving us. We shall never forget how he loved you."

"It will always be a very tender memory to me," Barbara replied and the tears of the two women flowed together, tears that brought comfort to them and at the same time united their sympathy for each other.

That evening, when Mr. Ward came up after his supper with Lewis (for Arthur had gone back to college), Mrs. Ward said, after expressing her thanks that she was recovering strength rapidly: "Richard, we owe Barbara a great deal for all she has done for us in our trouble. Isn't there something we can do to show it?"

"We certainly feel grateful to her," Mr. Ward said with thoughtful eagerness. "What do you think we can do?"

Mrs. Ward was silent a few moments.

"There's that money Aunt Wallace left you in trust two years ago to educate Carl when he should be ready to enter college." Mrs. Ward's voice faltered. "By the terms of the trust the money can now be used for any benevolent or philanthropic purpose. I have heard Barbara mention a plan that might succeed if it were wisely carried out. She thinks that, if a building were put up in

Crawford and dedicated to the training of young women for domestic service, preparing them for competent cooks and house-keepers, that a great deal might be done to elevate the labor of the kitchen and bring intelligent American girls into it. What do you think?"

"I think it is highly probable. At any rate, anything is preferable to the condition of things we endured before Barbara came. Anything is worth trying that will by any possibility tend to help matters."

"How much is Aunt Wallace's legacy?"

"It amounts to about fifteen hundred dollars now. That would not go far toward such a building as Barbara probably has in mind."

"No, but it would be a beginning, and I think I know where I could get more to go with it." Mrs. Ward was growing very much interested, and Mr. Ward was obliged to caution her against excitement; so the matter was dropped there.

But in a few days Mrs. Ward brought it up again in Barbara's presence.

"I think something could be done with a properly equipped building." Barbara said in answer to a question put by Mrs. Ward. They had discussed the matter several times before Mrs. Vane's invitation to Barbara to come to her evening gathering. Mrs. Ward had not yet hinted at any means for realizing such a project.

"How much do you suppose such a building would cost?" Mrs. Ward asked, noting Barbara's growing interest.

"Oh, I've no real idea. Almost any amount. It would cost a good deal to maintain it, also. The greatest difficulty would be to secure a proper person for superintendent."

"And then the next thing would be to get the girls to attend the housekeeping-school."

"I think I could find plenty of girls."

"I'm not so sanguine as you are, Barbara," Mrs. Ward answered slowly. "But Mr. Ward and I are willing to show our faith in such an attempt by giving two thousand dollars towards the erection of such a building.

She explained to Barbara Aunt Wallace's legacy, and added that Mr. Ward had offered to put five hundred dollars more with it to make it two thousand.

"I think Mrs. Vane and some of the other ladies in our church and society will give something, so that we can begin with a pretty good building and have enough to equip and run it. Suppose you go over and see Mrs. Vane some day this week, and have a talk with her about it."

"I will," said Barbara tingling with eagerness. Something real and tangible seemed about to come to pass in her career. She grew excited as she thought of possibilities. A building of the kind she had dreamed of was not by any means an answer to the servant-girl problem, but it was at least a real thing and if the idea was properly worked out it might result in great things.

So she talked with herself as she sung at her work that afternoon and resolved to go over to Mrs. Vane's at once, and yet even in the midst of her growing excitement and her genuine interest in her career Barbara was not altogether free from a depression that had its origin in the best feeling she had ever known. This feeling was her love for the minister, Mr. Morton. Barbara no longer tried to conceal from herself that he had become a real part of her life. The trouble in the Ward household had all tended indirectly to increase her admiration for him. With the tenderest sympathy he had entered into the family's grief. It was only natural that in the weeks that followed Carl's death Mr. Morton should call frequently at the house where he had become such a familiar guest in college days. Scarcely a day passed when he did not drop in for a meal, or to spend part of an evening.

In one way and another Barbara met him a good deal. He was always the same earnest, gentlemanly, kindly speaker and listener. Gradually in little moments of conversation when Mrs. Ward was not able to come down, and Mr. Ward and Morton had lingered over a little talk on social questions after tea, Barbara had taken an unconscious part in the discussion. More than once she had with almost guilty haste gone out of the sitting-room after one of those important discussions in which she had revealed a part of her ambitions to the young minister and Mr. Ward; and in the midst of her work, as she finished some kitchen task, she reproached her heart for yielding to what seemed like a hopeless affection. But the girl's life was opening into a full blossom under a power as old as the human race, as divine an instinct, as religious a hunger, as humanity ever knew. She was more than dimly conscious of all this, even in the midst of her self-reproaches.

But the consciousness of her position as a household servant and of his position as leader in the pulpit of the most influential church in Crawford was sharply painful. The gulf between them was not very deep personally. She was fully as well educated along lines of general culture. She was almost his equal in matters of knowledge and perception. It was the social distinction that separated them. And, as the days went by and she felt more and more the mental stimulus of his presence and the attractiveness of his manner towards her, she shrunk from the thought of the suffering in the future which she was making for herself in even allowing his life to become a part of hers.

All this was in her mind as she went over to see Mrs. Vane that afternoon. The new plan proposed by Mrs. Ward and the gift of the money to make it practical appealed to her ambition, and she resolutely set herself to satisfy herself with the working out of her ambitions for social service, saying to herself, not bitterly but sadly: "Barbara Clark, there is no place for love in the life you have chosen. Ambition is all you have any right to."

Ah; Barbara! Is that as far as you have gone in the school of life? There is nothing that can take love's place. For there is nothing greater in the kingdom of God. Ambition may keep you busy. It can never fill the place in your heart that God made to be filled.

She found Mrs. Vane as nearly disturbed as she had ever seen her. Generally the old lady was the personification of peace.

"What do you think?" was her greeting to Barbara the moment she entered the house. "Hilda has gone and got married! To a worthless young fellow after two months' acquaintance. The first I knew of it was this morning. It seems he persuaded her to marry him about a week ago. Today she says she must leave me to go and live with him. I don't blame her for that, but neither of them is fit to be married. Hilda has no more idea of what it means to make home than —"

Just then the bell rang, and Mrs. Vane went to the door. Barbara heard her talking earnestly to some one in the hall, and the next moment she came in, followed by Mr. Morton.

"Miss Clark, Mr. Morton," said the old lady, who seemed to enjoy Barbara's sudden coloring. "Mr. Morton thought he was interrupting some private conference if he came in. I don't know what you want, my dear; but I know Mr. Morton is interested in your plans, and he may be able to help in some way."

"Yes," replied Mr. Morton with a hesitation that Barbara had never noticed before in him, "I am truly interested in the problem Miss Clark is trying to work out. I don't know that I am competent to give advice in the matter. There are some subjects that even a young preacher just out of the seminary does not dare to face. I think the servant problem is one of them. I came in this afternoon, Mrs. Vane, to see if you could help me in the new social-settlement work we are planning for Marble Square Church."

"You want money out of me, young man. I see it in your face." Mrs. Vane gave him one of her sharpest looks. "Go to, now! It's shameful for a fine-looking young fellow like you to come here and wheedle a poor old woman like me out of her hard earned savings for your social experiments. Is that what you've come after too?" she suddenly asked, wheeling around toward Barbara.

"Yes," replied Barbara, laughing with Mr. Morton at Mrs. Vane's pretended anger. "I have no social settlements to beg for, but I want you to help me put up a building for training servants."

Mrs. Vane looked from Barbara to Mr. Morton and rubbed her nose vigorously.

"I believe you arranged this onslaught together. You conspired to combine your good looks and your blarney to rob me of necessities for old age."

"Indeed we did not, Mrs. Vane," replied Morton with a seriousness that Barbara thought unnecessary, knowing Mrs. Vane's manner as she did. "I know nothing of Mrs. Clark's plan. She came in first; and, if she gets all your money for her work, I won't complain."

"Get all you can, my dear," said Mrs. Vane grimly, turning to Barbara, who with real enthusiasm told the story of Mrs. Ward's proposed gift and the possibilities of such a building if rightly managed.

Mrs. Vane listened quietly until Barbara was through, and then said, "I'll give ten thousand dollars."

"Ten – ten – thou –" Barbara began trembling.

"I might as well go; you've got it all, Miss Clark," said Morton, rising with mock gravity.

"Sit down, sir!" said Mrs. Vane, while the sharp eyes twinkled at Barbara's confusion. "I said ten thousand. I don't think it's enough. I'll make it more after the building is up. You will need cooks and teachers and lot of help in every way. The thing will have to be endowed like a college. I see great possibilities in it. But I have never believed in scattering effort. What is the reason this building for the training of competent servants cannot be a part of the social settlement connected with the Marble Square Church? It is right in line with the rest of the things you propose, isn't it, Mr. Morton?"

Morton looked at Barbara, and Barbara glowed. Then she cast her eyes on the floor.

"Yes, I suppose such a building is in keeping with our social-settlement plans," Mr. Morton replied somewhat stiffly. "But Miss Clark probably wishes to work out her – plans – independently.'

"There's such a thing as being too independent!" quoth Mrs. Vane sharply.

"I suppose there is," answered Barbara faintly, and then sat silent. The thought of being in any sense connected with Mr. Morton gave her a feeling of bitter sweet.

"Well, think it over!" Mrs. Vane continued with what seemed like unnecessary sharpness. "I don't know but that I shall make the gift conditional on its being used in the social-settlement plan. So you needn't ask me for any money today, sir," she said, turning to Morton.

"Thank you, Mrs. Vane. I know how to take a hint," he replied gravely. And then he caught Barbara's look as she glanced up from the carpet, and his tone made Barbara laugh a little nervously. He joined in it, and Mrs. Vane kept them company.

"I don't know what the joke is about," she said at last, as she rubbed her nose again as if in disappointment.

"It's just as well, perhaps," Morton said. "Some jokes cannot be explained, not even by the makers of them."

He seemed to make no motion to go, and after a few minutes more of general talk about the proposed house, during which nothing more was said about the settlement, Barbara rose and said she must go, as she had some work to do before tea-time.

Mr. Morton instantly rose also.

"May I walk with you, Miss Clark? My calls take me your way."

"Certainly," Barbara murmured, and they went out together.

Mrs. Vane watched them from the window as they went past. The old lady was still rubbing her nose in some vexation.

"If he isn't thinking a good deal more of her than of the social settlement just now, then I'll give twenty thousand towards it instead of ten," she said, and then added: "They couldn't either of them do better. And if he doesn't have sense enough to know what is good for him, I'll try to help him out."

Barbara and Mr. Morton walked down the street, talking about everything except the proposed building and the social-settlement plans. After the first moment of embarrassment at the thought of walking with him had passed, Barbara was relieved to feel quite at her ease. She had never looked prettier. She had a gift of vivacious conversation. Mr. Morton was not her equal in that respect, but he was at his best when he had a good talker with him. They had just finished some innocent play at repartee and were laughing over it when, as they turned the corner towards the Wards, they met Mrs. Dillingham and her daughter.

Instantly Barbara's face became grave, and Mr. Morton as he raised his hat seemed equally sober. The Dillinghams passed them with what seemed to Barbara unusually severe faces. The light of the afternoon suddenly went out. She was no longer a college graduate, an educated young woman the equal, in everything but wealth, of this glorious creature she had just passed; she was only a hired girl, a servant. And the gulf that yawned between her and the minister was too deep to be bridged. It was folly to be happy any longer. Happiness was not for her; only ambition was left, and even that might not be possible if this social-settlement plan was to be involved in hers, and –"

"I beg pardon, Miss Clark, but did I hear you say the other night at Mrs. Vane's that you or your mother had known the Dillinghams before you came to Crawford?"

Mr. Morton was coming to the relief of her embarrassment.

"No, mother is related to one branch of the family. Mrs. Dillingham has been very kind to me since that evening," she added. "I have not been courteous, hardly, in response to her invitation."

"It's a very nice family," Mr. Morton said quite tamely.

"Yes, Miss Dillingham is a remarkably beautiful person, don't you think?" Barbara was not quite herself, or she would not have asked such a question.

"She is not as beautiful as some one else I know," replied Morton suddenly, and as he said it he looked Barbara full in the face.

It was one of those sudden yielding to temptation that the young minister in his singularly strong, earnest, serious life could number on his fingers. He regretted it the minute the words were spoken, but that could not recall them. Over Barbara's face the warm blood flowed in a deepening wave, and for a moment her heart stood still. Then, as she walked on, she was conscious of Mr. Morton's swiftly spoken apology as he noted her distress.

"Pardon me, Miss Clark. I forgot myself. I – will you forget – will you forgive me?"

Then Barbara had murmured some reply, and he had taken off his hat very gravely and bowed as he took leave of her, and she had gone on, with a flaming face and a beating heart.

"He asked me to forget it? I cannot," she said as she buried her face in her hands up in her room, while the tears wet her cheeks. "He asked me to forgive it. Forgive him for saying what he did? But it was not anything very dreadful." She smiled, then frowned at the recollection. "A silly compliment that gentlemen are in the habit of paying. But was it silly? Or was he in the habit of paying such? Was it not a real expression of what he felt –" She put her hand over her ears, as if to shut out whispers that might kill her ambitions and put something else in their place. But, when she went down to her work a little later, she could not shut out the picture of that afternoon. She could neither forget nor forgive. Oh Barbara! If he could only know how his plea for forgiveness was being denied; and with a smile, not a frown in the heart!

The rest of that week Mr. Morton stayed away from Mr. Ward's although Mr. Ward had expected him to tea on Friday. He sent a note pleading stress of church-work. Mr. Ward commented on it at the table.

"Morton is killing himself already. He seems to think he can do everything. He won't last out half his days at the present rate."

"He needs a good wife more than anything else," Mrs. Ward said carelessly. "Some one ought to manage him and tell him what to do."

"Yes, I suppose every woman in the church knows just the girl for him, and is ready to hint her name." Mr. Ward remarked.

"If he marries any one in Marble Square parish, it will create trouble. It always does," said Mrs. Ward.

"I think Morton has sense enough to look out for that," replied Mr. Ward briefly.

Barbara heard every word as she was serving at the table, and feared lest her face might betray her. But Mrs. Ward, in whom Barbara had never confided, as she had in Mrs. Vane, did not detect anything; and Barbara found relief by retiring soon to her kitchen.

The following Sunday she had an experience which added to her knowledge of the position she occupied as a servant, and led up to the great crisis of her life, as she will always regard it.

Since entering Mrs. Ward's family she had not attended evening service in any of the Crawford churches, owing to her desire to spend that time with her mother. But on this particular Sunday following her interview with Mrs. Vane and her talk with Mr. Morton she decided that she would go out to the Endeavor meeting at the Marble Square Church. There was no other service after the Christian Endeavor meeting on this Sunday evening, as it was the custom one Sunday in every month to give the whole evening to the society and its work. The minister was in the habit of attending this service and giving it his special notice, sometimes by making a direct address on the topic of the evening, or by taking a part assigned to him beforehand by the leader.

When Barbara went in that evening, the large, handsome chapel of the Marble Square Church was rapidly filling up. The talented, earnest, handsome young preacher was very popular with the young people, and the society had increased rapidly in membership and attendance since Morton's arrival.

The usher showed Barbara to a seat about halfway down the aisle. As she sat down, she noticed Mr. Morton talking with a group of young people down in front. When they separated, he looked up and saw her, and, coming down the aisle, he gravely shook hands, and then introduced her to the young woman next to her. He then went on to the door, greeted some of the members coming in, and then went around by a side aisle and sat down on a front seat just as the meeting began.

It had been a long time since Barbara had attended a Christian Endeavor meeting. She felt that she was growing rather old for it, but tonight she enjoyed it thoroughly. When the time came for Mr. Morton to speak, she was surprised to find how her anticipation of what he had to say was not spoiled by anything he said. It was all so manly, with such a genuine, real fragrance to it, so tinged with healthy humor, so helpful for real life, that it all helped her. She was grateful to him. Like the first sermon she had heard him preach, his talk tonight made her feel the value of life and the strength of effort in God's world.

Then suddenly, while she was looking at the earnest, eloquent face, the consciousness of the remoteness of his life from hers smote her into despair. When the service was over, she did not want to remain to the quiet, social gathering that followed. But her neighbor to whom Morton had introduced her asked her to come into the little gathering of other visitors and strangers who were being received by an introduction committee and made welcome to the society, the committee giving all strangers a topic, cards and other printed matter belonging to the society, and introducing them to one another as well as to members.

It was one of the new methods pursued by this committee to ask all strangers to sign a little card giving the address of the newcomer, so that some one of the society might call during the week, and, if necessary, act as escort to the next meeting. One of these cards was given to Barbara; and in a spirit of perversity, she signed her name and put under it the words, "House servant at Mr. Ward's, 36 Hamilton Street."

It was altogether unnecessary for her to be so ostentatious with her position; but she was not perfect, and felt an unnatural desire to test her reception right in Mr. Morton's own society. A few of the young people in the Marble Square Church knew who she was and what she was doing; and with a few exceptions she had been treated with great kindness, no discrimination whatever being made. But the majority of the young people did not know her; and tonight she was plainly dressed, her face was bearing the marks of the weariness of the strain of the last month's work, and it was not surprising that she was suspicious of every suggestion of a slight.

When the committee and the other strangers finally went out and mingled with the others in the large room, Barbara thought she detected a distinct coldness to her. She was certain her name and her position had been whispered around among the young people. As she afterward found out, she did the committee an injustice, as they had not told any one of her work. But she was left alone in the midst of all the others, and in spite of her habits of self-control and her previous experiences she began to feel a bitterness that was contrary to her sweet nature.

She looked around the room, and noticed Miss Dillingham talking with a group of older girls who had begun to come into the society a little while after Mr. Morton's call to Crawford; and she went over to her and spoke to her.

And then it was that Miss Dillingham, who was not perfect any more that Barbara, did as wrong a social act as she had ever done in her life. She simply nodded to Barbara without saying a word, and went on talking without introducing her friends to Barbara or taking any other notice of her.

Barbara instantly stepped back away from the group, while her face glowed and then paled. As she turned sharply around to go out of the door which was near, Mr. Morton confronted her. He had witnessed the little scene.

"You will always be welcome in our Endeavor Society, Miss Clark," he said, while the color that mounted to his face was as deep as hers.

"I shall never come again so long as I am a servant!" replied Barbara in a tone as near that of passion as she had ever shown him. And with the words she opened the door and went out into the night, leaving him standing there and looking at her with a look that would have made her tremble if she had lifted her face to his.

CHAPTER 7

We Cannot Choose in all Things.

WHEN Barbara went out into the darkness after that scene with Miss Dillingham, it was more than the darkness of physical night that oppressed her. She thought she realized with a vividness more real than she had ever before experienced the gulf that separated her from the young minister of Marble Square Church. With almost grim resolve she said to herself: "I have dreamed a vain dream. I will give myself up now to my career. Whatever ambition I have shall center about the possibilities of service. He can never be anything to me. It would risk all his prospects in life, even if – even if – he should come to care for me –" Her heart failed at the suggestion, for there had been intimations on the part of the young preacher that Barbara could not help interpreting to mean at least a real interest in her and her career.

"But no, it is not possible!" she said positively as she walked on. "His life is dependent on social conditions that he must observe. For him to ignore them must mean social loss and possibly social disgrace. The minister of Marble Square Church care for a hired girl! Make her his wife!" Barbara trembled at the thought of the sacred word which she hardly whispered to her heart. "Even if she were as well educated and well equipped for such a position as any young woman in his parish, still, nothing could remove the fact of her actual service." "And service," Barbara bitterly said to herself as she neared home, "service is no longer considered a noble thing. It is only beautiful young women like Miss Dillingham, who have nothing to do, who have the highest place in society. A girl who is really doing something with her hands to make a home a sweeter, more peaceful spot is not regarded by the world as worth more than any other cog in a necessary machine. Society cannot give real service any place in its worship. It is only the leisure of the idle wealth and fashion that wins the love and homage of the world."

"And the church too," Barbara continued her monologue after she had bidden her mother good night and gone up to her room, "The church, too, in its pride and vainglory is ready to join the world in scorn of honest labor of the hands." She recalled all the real and fancied slights and rebuffs she had endured in church and from church people since going out to service, and for a few minutes her heart was hard and bitter toward all Christian people. But gradually, as she grew quiet, her passion cooled, and she said to herself in a short prayer: "Lord, let me not offend by judging too hastily; and, if I am to lose out of my life my heart's desire for love, do not let me grow morose or chiding. Keep me sweet and uncomplaining. How else shall I help to make a better world?" A few tears fell as she prayed this prayer, and after a few minutes' quiet she felt more like her natural, even-tempered self.

"If I am going to stay a servant," she said with some calling back of her former habit, "I must learn what God thinks of service. I shall need all I can get out of His word to strengthen me in days to come." She had made a collection of her passages relating to service, and tonight she added to it from one of Paul's letters, dwelling on the words as she read them aloud:

"Servants, obey in all things your masters according to the flesh; not with eyeservice, as menpleasers; but in singleness of heart, fearing God: And whatsoever ye do, do it heartily, as to the Lord, and not unto men; Knowing that of the Lord ye shall receive the reward of the inheritance: for ye serve the Lord Christ. But he that doeth wrong shall receive for the wrong which he hath done: and there is no respect of persons. Masters, give unto your servants that which is just and equal; knowing that ye also have a Master in heaven." (Colossians 3:22 – 4:1)

"Of course," Barbara mused after saying the words, "all this was said to actual slaves, whose bodies were bought and sold in the market like cattle. But what wonderful words to be spoken to any class of servants either then or now! 'Whatsoever ye do, do it heartily!' One thing that servants lack in their service is heartiness. It is done for wages, not for love of service. 'As to the Lord, and not to men.' How few servants ever think of that! The Lord is the real master. He is being served if what I do is a good thing that needs doing. There is no respect of persons. How great a thing that is! In God's sight my soul is as much worth saving as any other. He thinks as much of me as He does of the rich and the famous. 'Masters, give unto your servants that which is just and equal.' If that were done, it might make conditions far different so far as the servant-girl question is concerned. But who will tell us what is meant by 'just and equal' today?" Barbara shook her head doubtfully, and went on. " 'Knowing that your Master also is in heaven.' That helps me. Paul must have known my need as well as the need of the poor bond-servants to whom he wrote. 'A Master in heaven.' May He help me to serve Him in spirit and in truth."

So Barbara the next day did not present the appearance of the modern broken hearted-heroine in the end-of-the-century novel. Any one who knew her could plainly see marks in her face and manner of a great experience. But there was no gloom about her, no un-Christian tragic bewailing of fate or circumstance. If she were to live her life as she supposed she should, without life's greatest help to live, so far as human love can go, she would at least live it bravely as so many other souls have done. And yet, Barbara, you know well enough that Ambition does not spell Love. And, in spite of all, you know your heart would tremble if the young minister of Marble Square Church should pass you and give you one earnest look out of his great dark eyes, as he did on that well-remembered day when he said that you were beautiful. Ah, Barbara! Are you quite sure you have forever bidden farewell to the holiest dream of your womanhood?

She busied herself during the day with her work, and in the evening went over to Mrs. Vane's to see her again concerning the proposed building. She was eager to get to work. Her heart longed for busy days to keep her mind absorbed.

Mrs. Vane suggested several good ideas.

"While you are waiting to complete the details of the building itself, why not interview a large number of factory and store girls about their work? Find out something about the reasons that appeal to young women for a choice of labor. You are not certain that you can get any girls to attend your training-school. I think you can, but very many other good people will tell you your plan is senseless. It is only when people begin to try to do good in the world that they discover what fools they are. Other people who never make an effort to better the world will tell them so. There will arise a host of tormenting critics as soon as the idea of your proposed training-school is suggested. They will tear it all to pieces. Don't pay any attention to them. The world does not owe anything to that kind of criticism. But it will help your plan if before the building is put up you can answer honest questions as to its practical working. There's another thing I would like to say; and I shall say it, my dear, seeing I am old enough to be your grandmother."

"What's that?" Barbara asked, coloring. She anticipated Mrs. Vane's next remark.

"I think it would be a distinct saving of power if in some way we could make the training-school a part of Mr. Morton's social-settlement work."

"I don't think it is possible," replied Barbara in a low voice. Her manner expressed so much distress that the old lady said at once: "My dear, I will not say any more about it. But will you permit me to tell you plainly that I am firmly convinced that Mr. Morton is in love with you, and will ask you to marry him, and you will have to give him some kind of a satisfactory answer, for he is not a young man to be satisfied with unsatisfactory answers."

"Oh, I cannot believe it!" Barbara exclaimed, and then she put her face in her hands, while she trembled.

"It's true!" the old lady said sturdily. "My old eyes are not so dim that I cannot see love talking out of other eyes. And that is what his were saying when he was here last week. My dear, there is nothing dreadful about it. I should enjoy having you for my pastor's –"

"But it is impossible –" Barbara lifted her head blushingly.

"There is nothing impossible in Love's kingdom," replied the old lady gently. If it comes to you, do not put it away. You are his equal in all that is needful for your happiness.

Then Barbara told her all about the event of the night before at church. If she had been a Catholic, she would have gone to a priest. Being a Protestant, she confessed to this old lady, because her heart longed for companionship, and there was that quality in Mrs. Vane which encouraged confidences.

When she was through, Mrs. Vane said: "There is nothing very hopeless about all this. He has certainly never been anything but the noble-hearted Christian gentleman in his treatment of you." (Barbara did not tell of the remark Mr. Morton had made about beautiful faces. But inasmuch as he had apologized for a seeming breach of gentlemanly conduct, she did not feel very guilty in withholding the incident from Mrs. Vane.) "And I really believe he feels worse than you do over any slights you received from the members of the church."

Barbara was silent. Now that her heart was unburdened she felt grateful to Mrs. Vane, but she naturally shrank from undue expression of her feelings. Mrs. Vane respected her reserve as she had encouraged her confidence.

"Don't be downhearted, my dear. Go right on with your plans. Count on me for the ten thousand and more if the plan develops as I think it will. And meanwhile, if in your trips among the working girls, you run across any one who can take Hilda's place, send her around. I haven't been able to find anybody yet. I would get along without help, but Mr. Vane will not allow it, with all the company we have. No, don't shake hands like men. Kiss me, my dear."

So Barbara impulsively kissed her, and went away much comforted. She dreaded the thought that she might meet the young minister, and half hoped she might. But for the next three weeks Mr. Morton was called out of Crawford on a lecture tour which the Marble Square Church granted him; and, when Barbara learned that he was gone, she almost felt relieved as she planned her work with Mrs. Ward's hearty cooperation to see as many working girls as possible for information, and to learn from them the story of their choice of life labor, and its relation to her own purpose so far as helping the servant question was concerned.

What Barbara learned during the next three weeks would make a volume in itself. She did not know that she had any particular talent for winning confidences, but a few days' experience taught her that she was happily possessed of a rare talent for making friends. She managed in one way and other to meet girls at work in a great variety of ways. In the big department store of Bondman's & Co., in the long row of factories by the river, in the girls' refreshment rooms at the Young Women's Christian Association, in the office of business friends where the click of the typewriter was the constant note of service, in the restaurants and waiting-rooms about the big union station, in the different hotels and a few of the boarding-houses of Crawford, Barbara met representatives of the great army of young women at work in the city; and out of what seemed like meager and unsatisfactory opportunities for confidence and the sharing of real purpose in labor she succeeded in getting much true information, much of which shaped her coming plan and determined the nature of her appeal to the mistresses on one hand, and the servant on the other.

"With a few exceptions then," she said to Mrs. Ward one evening after she had been at work on this personal investigation for three weeks, "all this army of girls at work represents a real need in the home somewhere. I found some girls working in the offices, and a very few in the stores and factories, who said they were working for other reasons than for necessary money. Here is a list of girls in Bondman's. I told them I did not want it for the purpose of printing it, and it is not necessary. But there are over two hundred of these girls who cannot by any possibility save any money out of their expenses, and a few of them" – Barbara spoke with a sense of shame for her human kind and of indignation against un-Christian greed in business – "a few of them hinted at temptations to live wrong lives in order to earn enough to make them independent. And yet all of these girls vigorously refused to accept a position offered to leave the store and go to work at double the wages in a home as a servant. I offered over fifty of these girls four dollars a week and good board and room at Mrs. Vane's, and not one of them was willing to accept it, even when, as in many cases, they were not receiving over three and a half a week, out of which they had to pay for board and other necessaries."

"And the reason they gave was?" Mrs. Ward, who was an interested listener, asked the question.

"They hated the drudgery and confinement of house labor. They loved the excitement and independence of their life in the store. Of course, they all gave as one main reason for not wanting to be house servants the loss of social position. Several of the girls in the factory had been hired girls. They all without exception spoke of their former work with evident dislike, and with one or two exceptions refused to entertain any proposition to go back to the old work. I think one of the girls in the Art mills will go to Mrs. Vane's. She worked for her some years ago, and liked her. But what can the needs of the home of today present to labor in the way of inducement to come into its field? I must confess I had very little to say to the girls in the way of inducement. Not on account of my own experience," Barbara hastened to say with a grateful look at Mrs. and Mr. Ward, "for you have been very, very kind to me and made my service sweet; but in general, I must confess, after these three weeks' contact with labor outside the home, I see somewhat more clearly the reason why all branches of woman's labor have inducements that house labor does not offer."

"And how about the prospects for pupils for the training-school?" Mr. Ward asked keenly. He had come to have a very earnest interest in the proposed building.

"Out of all the girls I have seen," Barbara answered with some hesitation, "only four have promised definitely that they would take such a course and enter good homes as servants. One of these was an American girl in an office. The others were foreign-born girls in Bondman's."

"The outlook is not very encouraging, is it?" Mrs. Ward remarked with a faint smile.

"It looks to me, Martha," Mr. Ward suggested, "as if it might be necessary to put up a training-school for training our Christian housekeepers as well as Christian servants. If what Barbara has secured in the way of confession from these girls is accurate, it looks as if they are unwilling to work as servants because of the unjust or unequal or un-Christian conditions in the houses that employ them."

"At the same time, Richard, remember the great army of incompetent, ungrateful girls we have borne with here in our home for years until Barbara came. What can the housekeeper do with such material? If the girls were all like Barbara, it would be different, you know."

"Well, I give it up," replied Mr. Ward with a sigh as he opened up his evening paper. "The whole thing is beyond me. And Barbara, of course, will be leaving us as soon as this new work begins. And then farewell to peace, and welcome chaos again."

"You are not going to leave us just yet are you, Barbara?" Mrs. Ward asked with an affectionate glance at Barbara.

"The house is not built yet," Barbara answered, returning Mrs. Ward's look.

"Of course, Barbara will leave us when she has a home of her own," Mr. Ward said in short sentences as he read down a part of the page. "Then our revenge for her leaving us will be the thought that her troubles have just begun when she begins to have hired girls herself."

"I don't think there's any sign of it yet," Mrs. Ward said, looking keenly at Barbara, who colored a little, "I have not noticed any beaus in the kitchen."

"More likely to come in through the parlor," Mr. Ward suggested. And again Barbara looked up with a blush, and Mrs. Ward could not help admiring the girl's pure, intelligent face.

There was silence for a moment while Barbara went over her list of figures and memoranda.

"I see Morton is back from the West," Mr. Ward suddenly exclaimed, looking up from his paper. "The News says he had a remarkable tour, and prints a large part of his recent address on the temperance issue. I predict for him a great career. Marble Square never did a wiser thing than when it called him to its pulpit. My only fear is that he may kill himself with these lecture tours."

There was silence again, and Barbara bent her head a little lower over her work, which lay on the table.

"He is certainly a very promising young man," Mrs. Ward said, and just then the bell rang.

"Shouldn't wonder if that was Morton himself," Mr. Ward exclaimed as he rose. "I asked him to come in and see us as soon as he came back. I'll go to the door."

He went out into the hall and opened the door, and Mrs. Ward and Barbara could hear him greet Mr. Morton, speaking his name heartily.

"Come right into the sitting-room, Morton. We're there to-night. Mrs. Ward will be delighted to see you."

Barbara rose and slipped out into the kitchen just as Mr. Ward and Morton reached the end of the hall.

She busied herself with something there for half an hour. At the end of that time she heard Mr. Ward's hearty, strong voice saying good-night to Morton as he went out into the hall with him.

After a few minutes Barbara came back into the sitting room and taking her list of names and facts from the table prepared to go up to her room.

Mr. Ward was saying as she came in, "Morton seemed very dull for him, don't you think?"

"He is probably very tired with his lecture tour. It is a very exhausting sort of –"

The front door opened quickly; a strong, firm step came through the hall; and Mr. Morton opened the sitting-room door and stepped in.

"Excuse me, Ward, I left my gloves on the table," he began as he walked in. Then he saw Barbara, who had turned as he entered.

"I'm glad to see you Miss Clark," he said as he picked up his gloves; and then he added, as he remained somewhat awkwardly standing in the middle of the room, "How is your training-school building getting on? I suppose it is hardly finished yet?"

Barbara made some sort of answer, and Mrs. Ward added a word about what Barbara had been doing while Mr. Morton had been gone.

Morton expressed his interest in some particular item of information given by Mrs. Ward, and told a little incident that had come under his own observation during his lecture tour.

Mr. Ward asked a question suggested by something the young minister had said, and that seemed to remind him of a story he had heard on the train. Before anyone realized exactly how it happened, Morton was seated, talking in the most interesting manner about his trip. He had a keen sense of humor, and some of the scenes he had witnessed while on his tour were very funny as he told them. Barbara found herself laughing with an enjoyment she had not felt for a long time. She was delighted with Morton's powers of dramatic description and the apparently unfailing fund of anecdote that he possessed. She wondered at his remarkable memory, and her wonder was evidently shared by Mr. and Mrs. Ward who had long thought Morton a marvel in that respect.

In the midst of a most interesting account of the way he had been introduced to a Western audience by a local character, a neighboring clock in one of the city buildings struck ten.

Morton stopped talking and rose.

"I had no idea it was so late. Pardon me." He said good-night somewhat abruptly, and started for the door.

"You're sure you haven't left anything this time?" asked Mr. Ward.

"I have, though," Mr. Morton answered with some confusion, as he came back to the table and took up his hat, which he had dropped there when he took up his gloves. As he did so, he glanced at Barbara, who lowered her eyes and turned towards the kitchen as if to go out.

"I get more absent-minded every day," he said somewhat feebly.

"You need a wife to look after you," said Mrs. Ward with decision. She had picked up her work, which she had dropped in her lap while Morton was telling stories, and was intent on finishing it.

Barbara opened the kitchen door, and went out just as Mr. Ward said with a laugh, "Probably every woman in Marble Square Church has some particular wife in view for you, and you will disappoint all of them when you finally make a choice without consulting them."

"I probably shall," replied Morton quietly, and, saying good-night again, he went away.

Mr. Ward was silent a few minutes, and then said, as if he had been thoughtfully considering a new idea: "Morton didn't seem at all dull or tired after coming back for his gloves. Have you thought that there might be a reason for it?"

"No. What reason?" Mrs. Ward looked up suddenly from her work, startled by Mr. Ward's manner.

"I think he enjoys Barbara's company."

"Richard Ward! You don't mean to say that Ralph Morton would marry Barbara!"

"I not only think he would; I think he will," replied Mr. Ward quietly.

Mrs. Ward was too much surprised at the unexpected suggestion to offer a word of comment at first. The thought of such a thing was so new to her that she had been totally unprepared for it.

"How would you like to have Barbara for your minister's wife?" Mr. Ward asked in the bantering tone he sometimes used.

Mrs. Ward was on the point of replying a little sharply. But suffering had done its mellowing work in her life. Before Carl's death she would have resented as an unparalleled impossibility such a thought as that of the pastor of the Marble Square Church choosing for his wife even a girl like Barbara, his intellectual and Christian equal. But many things since Barbara's coming into the home had conspired to change Mrs. Ward's old habits. And, as Mr. Ward asked his question now, she saw a picture of Barbara and Carl as they had been one evening a few days before the child's death. His little arms were about Barbara's neck, and his pale, thin cheek was lying close against hers.

"If it should come to that," she finally answered Mr. Ward's question slowly, "I am sure there is one woman in the Marble Square Church who will not make any trouble."

Mr. Ward looked surprised. But, as he went out into the front hall to lock the door for the night, he muttered, "A man can never tell what a woman will say or do when she is struck by lightning."

During the week that followed Barbara spent all the time she was able to spare from her own work in securing facts connected with her proposed plans. Mrs. Ward herself went with her to several well-known houses in Crawford, and introduced her to her friends. In every instance Barbara found there was the greatest possible interest in the subject, but no two women seemed to agree as to any policy or plan. There was unanimous agreement on one thing; namely, a need of capable, intelligent, honest servants in the house, who were to be depended on for continuous service, or for at least a period of several years that might be reckoned as continuous, the same as a business man could count on the continuous service in his employ of a competent bookkeeper or clerk who was necessary to the welfare of the business, but no more so than a competent servant in continuous service is necessary to the welfare of the home.

"The trouble is," one woman after another would say, "in the girls themselves. They do not have any ambitions as a class. They do not wish to be taught. They resent advice. They are ungrateful for nearly all favors. They do not thank anybody to try to improve their condition. We are tired of constant efforts made to solve an unsolvable problem with the material that must be used."

Still, in spite of all discouragements, Barbara bravely determined to go on, and her next effort was directed toward the girls who had expressed a willingness to go into service in the home instead of the store and factory.

She managed to call all these together Saturday evening at her own home and with her mother helping her she made a pleasant evening, serving some light refreshments and entertaining the girls with music and pictures.

There were eight of them in all. Two of them had had a little experience at house service. None of them, Barbara found on questioning, was really competent to manage the affairs of a household. Two were American girls who had lived on farms, and had come into Crawford to accept small places at Bondman's. Their experiences there had not been pleasant, and they were ready to try something that promised at least a temporary financial relief.

Barbara gave a little impromptu talk before the girls went home, and ended it by asking the girls to ask questions or talk over in a general way the prospects of housekeeping service as she had described it to them.

"Do you think, Miss Clark, from your own experience, that the hired girl's loss of social standing is the one great obstacle to the settlement of the question of service?" one of the American girls asked. She was a bright-looking girl, evidently a lover of fine looking dresses, and, as Barbara had discovered, with habits of extravagance far beyond her little means to gratify.

Barbara hesitated a moment before she answered.

"Yes, I think perhaps that is the most serious factor in the problem. I don't consider it unanswerable. I believe that Christian housekeepers and Christian servants can find an answer that will satisfy them both."

"I think the irregular hours are the hardest part of housework," said one of the girls, an honest-faced German, somewhat older than the others. "I worked two years for a family in the West, and some days I did not get through with my work until nine and even ten o'clock at night. One reason I have liked the store is because the hours of labor have been regular. I know just exactly how long I have to work. But I cannot earn enough where I now am. I saved over one hundred and fifty dollars one year when I was working out at four dollars a week."

"It's the dirty work that I don't like," spoke up a careless-looking girl whom Barbara had found in the bundle department at Bondman's. Barbara did not know just what it was that had drawn this girl to her; but something had done it, and there was something very attractive about Barbara to the girl, and she had expressed a certain readiness to learn the work of a servant so as to be competent.

"That never troubled me any," said the neatest girl of all. "My trouble was caused by not knowing how to do the work satisfactorily. I found I did not know how to plan for the meals and cook them properly. One of my friends, who was in the next house, was a splendid cook and manager. It was a large family, but she seemed to throw the work off easily because she knew how to plan it right."

"That's it!" Barbara spoke eagerly. "Is it any wonder that so many women complain at the troubles they have with servants when so many of them have no experience, and yet claim as high wages as if they had? A bookkeeper would not expect to get and retain a place in a business firm if he did not understand the business of keeping books; yet the housekeepers tell me that girls are continually coming into their houses, claiming to be competent for the work when in reality they do not know anything about it. It is necessary for the girls to put themselves in the places of the housekeepers, and ask, What should I have a right to expect from a girl who came into my house as a servant?"

"There's another thing I hear other girls complain about," said one of the older of the company. "They say that in most families the scale of wages paid to servants never changes. They say they never get any more a week after years of working out than they got when they begun. I know one girl who has been with one family five years. The first year she had two dollars and seventy-five cents. The third year they increased her wages to three and a half for fear of losing her, and they have remained at that figure ever since. Girls who work out do not have the ambition to get on that young men in a business firm have. They cannot look forward to a better condition or higher pay."

"That isn't true in some families I know," replied Barbara. "I know some people in Crawford who offer increased wages for increased ability or length of time the girls stay with them. Of course, we have to remember that most people who hire labor for the house claim that they can afford to pay only about so much for such work. The woman who lives next to Mrs. Ward complains because Mrs. Ward gives me four dollars and a half a week. The other woman says she is unable to pay so much; but all her girls, when they hear what I am getting, want as much, whether they are capable of earning it or not. Then, because she cannot pay it, they become dissatisfied and leave her. I am afraid Mrs. Ward has made an enemy out of a neighbor on my account, by paying me what she thinks I am worth."

"Don't you think you are entitled to the four and a half?" asked the careless-looking girl.

"Indeed I do," replied Barbara, laughing. "I think I earn every cent of it."

"Then I don't see what right the other woman has to find fault with Mrs. Ward for paying it."

"I don't, either," said Barbara frankly. "But perhaps the whole question of wages belongs to the question of ability. I don't think though, that we need to talk so much about that as about the need of a true thought of what service means. There is practically no ideal of service in the minds of most girls today.

To serve is to follow Christ, who was a servant. To serve a family, to minister to its necessary physical wants, to do drudgery in the name of God, to keep on faithfully every day in the line of duty, working cheerfully, heartily, washing dishes clean, sweeping rooms without shirking, learning the best ways to prepare food for the household – all this is a part of a noble life, and it is this thought of the dignity and nobility of service that is lost out of the world today. It must be recovered before we can begin to solve the question. There must be on the part of the mothers and housekeepers and on the part of the girls who consecrate themselves to home ministry a real thought of the real meaning of a servant's place in the economy of life. The homes of America must learn to sanctify and beautify the labor of the hands. Not until our social Christianity has learned the lesson of ministry, and learned that it is as noble to minister in the kitchen as in the pulpit, not until then shall we begin to have any answer worth having to the question of service in the home."

Barbara stopped suddenly and then said with a smile at the little group: "But this is a long sermon for Saturday night, and see how late it is! I can't ask you to stay any longer. But I want you to come again."

The careless-looking girl was the last to say good-night. As she shook Barbara's hand strongly, she said, "I don't think the sermon was too long, Miss Clark. I don't go to church on Sunday, and I need preaching. I think maybe I owe you more than you imagine."

To Barbara's surprise the girl suddenly threw an arm about her neck and kissed her. There was a tear on her cheek as she suddenly turned and went down the steps and joined the others.

"If I have such an influence over that soul, my Lord," prayed Barbara that night, "help me to use it for her salvation." It was already becoming a sweet source of satisfaction to Barbara that the ambition of her life was beginning to mean a saving of other lives. She was only yet dimly conscious of her great influence over other girls.

The next day was Sunday, and she remembered her foolish remark to Mr. Morton. During all his absence she had not been to the Marble Square Church services. She had attended elsewhere, but had not been out in the evening, going to her mother's and spending the evening reading to her. She had at present Rev. F. B. Meyer's book, "The Shepherd Psalm," and both mother and daughter were enjoying it very much.

She was reading the last chapter, and even as she read she remembered that this was the night when the Christian Endeavor Society at the Marble Square Church had the entire service. There was no preaching after the Endeavor meeting, which closed about eight o'clock.

It was half-past eight as Barbara finished the beautiful narrative, and her mother had thanked her and made some comment on the clearness of the style and its spiritual helpfulness, when the bell rang.

They had so few visitors, especially on Sunday, that they were startled by the sound. But Barbara rose at once and went to the door.

When she opened it, she uttered an exclamation of astonishment. For Mr. Morton was standing there! His face was pale and even stern, Barbara imagined, as he stood there.

"May I come in?" he said quietly, as Barbara stood still. "I want very much to see you and your mother."

Barbara murmured a word of apology, and then invited him to enter. Mrs. Clark rose to greet him, and the minister took the seat she proffered to him.

CHAPTER 8

Ministry is Divine.

MR. MORTON broke a very embarrassing silence by saying in a very quiet voice, although his manner showed still the great excitement that he evidently felt, "Mrs. Clark, I have no doubt you are greatly surprised to see me here."

"It is a great pleasure, I am sure," Mrs. Clark murmured. Barbara had turned around so that the young minister could not see her face as she sat partly concealed behind the lamp on the table. It was very still again before Mr. Morton spoke.

"You know, of course, that I have no preaching service to-night. I have just come from my young people's meeting. I –"

He paused, and Mrs. Clark looked attentively at him and then at Barbara sitting with head bowed and cheeks flushed, and a gleam of sudden perception of the truth began to shine out of the mother's face as she turned again toward the minister. Barbara had never confided directly in her mother, but Mrs. Clark had been blessed with a remarkably beautiful and true love experience in her own girlhood, and with all her faults and misunderstanding of Barbara during the trial of her experiment with Mrs. Ward she had in various ways come to know that Barbara had grown to have much interest in the brilliant young preacher. Barbara had probably made a serious mistake in not giving her mother a frank confession. But Mrs. Clark had never really supposed until now that the minister might have a feeling for Barbara as he stopped suddenly.

"We are very glad to see you, I am sure," Mrs. Clark said, coming to his rescue. Through the memory of her own sad loss and all her recent trouble rose the sweet picture of her husband's wooing. If Barbara's happiness for life now consisted in her possible union with this good, strong man, Mrs. Clark was not the mother to put needless obstacles in the way. In this matter her mother had a certain largeness of character which Barbara did not at that time comprehend.

Mr. Morton had grown calmer. He began to talk of matters belonging to his church and his plans for the social settlement. Gradually Barbara recovered herself from the first moment's panic. She came out from behind the defense of the lamp, and began to ask questions and take part in the conversation.

"But still," she was saying after half an hour's talk had been going on, "I do not quite see how you are going to interest Crawford people in the plan you suggest until you have made a practical beginning, even if it is on a small scale. The people are very conservative."

"That's true." The minister sighed a little. "But I do not see how you are going to interest the public in your servant girl's training-school until you have demonstrated its practical usefulness. I don't doubt its wisdom, of course," he added quickly. "But it must require a good deal of courage on your part to make a beginning in view of what you know must be the criticism and prejudice that are inevitable."

"As far as courage goes," said Barbara frankly, "it seems to me you have much more than I. With the money Mrs. Ward and Mrs. Vane have promised me, I shall be quite independent to work out my plan as I please. Whereas you are obliged to overcome the prejudice of a whole church full of people, many of whom do not believe in social-settlement work connected with the church."

"I wish there was some way," Mr. Morton exclaimed eagerly, absorbed in thought of his plans, "in which we could combine your plans and mine. The training-school would fit in so beautifully with my ideas."

He spoke with enthusiasm, for the moment, thinking only of the plans as existing apart from the persons. But, as Barbara lifted her face to his and then dropped her eyes, while a great wave of color swept her cheeks, he realized how personal his exclamation had been.

And just at the juncture, Mrs. Clark, without a word of apology or explanation, rose and walked out of the room. Morton blessed her as he shut the door. There are some things in the love chapter of youth that cannot be told except to the heart of youth itself.

He went quickly over to where Barbara was seated on the other side of the table, and before she had time to be frightened he said, looking at her with love's look: "Barbara, I love you, and want you to be my wife and share all with me. Will you?"

Barbara sat all in a tumult, her heart beating fast, as in a dream wondering at it all. And it sounded very sweet to her. For she loved him truly. But she said, as she stood by the table looking at him: "But – I – cannot. It would be –"

"Tell me, Barbara," he said, a sudden smile lighting up his pale face, and his use of her name was again music to her, "tell me only one thing first. Do you love me?"

"Yes!" she cried, and it seemed to her as if one person in her had spoken to another, compelling the answer; and the next moment, she could not realize how, but it was like a world's life to her, his arms were about her, and in that moment she knew that for better, for worse, she had put her life into the lot of sharing with his.

Lovers do not count time like other people. After a while he was saying: "But tell me, Barbara, how I am to make my peace with Mrs. Ward. For, when she learns that I am going to get her hired girl, she will never forgive me."

Then Barbara's face grew grave.

"Do you realize, Mr. Morton, what you have done? Can a young man with your position and prospects afford – to – to marry a 'hired girl'? Oh if you had not compelled me to say, 'Yes' so soon! I might have saved you from making the mistake of your life –"

"Barbara," he answered, with sudden sternness that was assumed, without answering her question. "If you ever call me 'Mr. Morton' again, I shall –" he left his threat unfinished; but he had possession of her hand as he spoke, and Barbara looked up at him and said softly, "What shall I call you?"

"Say –"

"Yes. What?" Barbara asked innocently, as he paused.

"Will you repeat after me?"

"Yes," she replied incautiously.

"Well then," he went on joyously, "say: 'Ralph, I love you more than any one else in the world. And I will walk with you through life because I love you – because we love each other.'"

"You have taken advantage of me!" she exclaimed brightly, and then, with glowing face looking into his, she repeated the words, whispering them. And, when she had finished, they were both reverently silent, while her eyes were wet with tears of solemn joy. They did not either of them realize all they had pledged to each other; but the God-given, human-divine love was upon them, and the blessedness of it swallowed up all fears of the future. Once Barbara had given herself to him, it meant an end of doubt or fear. She might discuss with him the probable results to his social or professional standing, but she would never torture his mind or distress her own by vain regrets or foolish anticipations. The great truth of their love for each other filled them both.

They were so absorbed in their talk that they did not hear Mrs. Clark when she came into the room. Then Mr. Morton was suddenly aware of her presence, and he instantly rose and went over to her.

"Mrs. Clark," he said, "I took advantage of your absence to take your daughter from you. But I will try to make up for it in part by giving you a loving and dutiful son, if you will accept me as such."

Without waiting for her reply, which he easily read in her smiling face, he turned to Barbara who had come to his side.

"What did you say, Barbara?" Mrs. Clark asked as she faced them both, thinking to herself that she had never seen so much real joy in two faces anywhere in the world.

"Oh mother!" Barbara cried, "I have given him my answer." She laid her head on her mother as she used to do when she was a little girl, and Mrs. Clark felt with the painful joy of a good mother's heart, that the world's old story had come into her daughter's life, and that henceforth this man had become to Barbara all in all without displacing the mother from her rightful share of affection.

They had many things to say now, and neither Barbara nor Mrs. Clark offered serious objections to the earnest request of the young man that the period of engagement might be a brief one.

"We know our minds quite well, I am sure," he said, while Barbara, blushing, nodded yes. "It will be best in every way for us to begin our home very soon. Barbara, you will have to give Mrs. Ward notice that you must leave. Poor Mrs. Ward! She is the only person I am sorry for right now."

They were all silent for a moment. Then Mr. Morton said, "The servant's training-school will have to be a part of the social settlement now. You've lost your independence."

"I've gained something better," said Barbara gently. Her love knew no restrictions, now that it was returned, and her heart leaped up to his in all his ambitions for helping to make a better world.

When he rose to go, Barbara went to the door with him. He had opened it, and was about to step out, when he turned and said with a laugh, "I have forgotten my hat."

The missing hat was not found at once, and Mrs. Clark unblushingly said, "Perhaps it is in the sitting-room," and walked deliberately out there.

The hat was lying on a chair behind the table. The minister took it up and walked to the door again. Then he turned and said, while Barbara looked up at him, "I forgot something else."

Then he stooped and kissed her, and went out into the night, and it was like the glory of heaven's brightness all about him, while Barbara turned and again met her mother with an embrace where both mingled their tears over the divine romance of this earthly life. God bless the repetition of the pure love chapter in human hearts. When it is deeply Christian as in the case of Barbara and Ralph, it is approved of Christ and has the sanction of all heaven.

When Barbara began her work at the Wards' next day, she had a natural dread of breaking the news to Mrs. Ward. But that lady unconsciously made a good opportunity. She came into the kitchen early in the forenoon, and was struck by Barbara's beauty. She had noted it many times before, but this morning the girl's great love experience had given her face an additional charm. It is no wonder Ralph Morton fell in love with her. He said it all began from that Sunday when he first met her at the Marble Square Church.

"Why Barbara," Mrs. Ward exclaimed, "you look perfectly charming this morning. How do you manage to keep looking so lovely? It is a wonder to me that the kitchen is not full of beaus all the time!"

Barbara laughed lightly. "I don't want a kitchen full of beaus. One is enough."

Mrs. Ward looked at her attentively. Then she said somewhat gravely: "Did you say one is enough? What does that mean?"

"It means – Oh Mrs. Ward, I am so happy!" She turned to her, and the other woman trembled a little and then said, "It is Mr. Morton?"

"Yes," cried Barbra, and Mrs. Ward put her arms about her and kissed her. Then she stepped back, and looked at her somewhat sorrowfully.

"I'm glad for you, of course, but what are we going to do? It's always this way. The best girls I have always go and get married. But I never thought until lately that you would do such a thing. Why, it's like a story, Barbara. If it was in a book, people would think it was quite improbable. 'The idea!' they would say, 'of the brilliant young preacher of Marble Square Church, Crawford, the gifted young writer and lecturer, marrying a hired girl in his own parish!' Have you thought, Barbara, of the sensation this event will make in Marble Square Church?"

"Of course I have not had much time yet to think of it Mrs. Ward. If Mr. Morton, Ralph," she added shyly, blushing at her use of the name before another person, "if he feels satisfied, the church ought not to give any trouble. Why should it? Do you think it will?"

"You're a hired girl in the eyes of most people in the church. They do not know you as I do. I am afraid it will make trouble for Mr. Morton."

For a moment Barbara's radiant face showed signs of anxiety. Then to Mrs. Ward's astonishment she said with a smile: "I am not going to borrow trouble over it. I love him too much to be afraid of anything."

"If only people knew you as Mr. Ward and I do –" Mrs. Ward faltered, tears in her eyes, caused by affection for Barbara and sorrow at the thought of losing her out of the home. But I don't know what Mrs. Rice and Mrs. Wilson and Mrs. Brown will say."

"Do you know –" Barbara spoke, not flippantly, but with a sense of happy humor which was a real part of her healthy nature, "Do you know Mrs. Ward, I am afraid I am not quite so much in fear of what Mrs. Rice and Mrs. Wilson and Mrs. Brown will say as I ought to be? I am not going to marry them, but – but – some one else."

Mrs. Ward looked at her doubtfully. Then she smiled at her and said: "You must be very much in love, Barbara. The old adage, 'Love laughs at locksmiths,' will have to be changed to 'Love laughs at Marble Square Church.'"

"I don't laugh at it, Mrs. Ward. But honestly, I do not feel to blame, and I am not going to anticipate trouble. That would not be right towards him, for I know he counted all the cost before he asked me to share all with him."

Blessed be love like Barbara's! Truly can it be said of such love, it "beareth all things, believeth all things, hopeth all things, endureth all things. Love never faileth."

When Mr. Ward came home at night, he soon learned the news. Barbara had no silly or false sentiment, and she agreed with Mr. Morton that the fact of their engagement and near marriage need not be kept secret from any one, even for a short time. So Mrs. Ward told her husband. He was not surprised. He had anticipated it.

"Yes, you're going to leave us, just like all the rest," he said in his bantering fashion, when Barbara came in with some dishes to set the table. Mr. Ward was in the reading-room, and Barbara stepped to the door and greeted him. "One of the rules of your new training-school ought to be, 'No girl who graduates from this school to go out to service shall be allowed to get engaged or married for at least five years.' What is going to become of all the competent girls if they all follow your bad example?"

"I'm sure I don't know," Barbara answered demurely.

"Won't you and Morton take us in to board when you begin housekeeping? I'm so used to your cornbread muffins and coffee for breakfast that I know I shall never be able to put up with any other kind."

"I don't know," Barbara replied laughing. "It is possible that we may have a hired girl ourselves."

"Do you think so?" Mr. Ward said with pretended joy. "Then Mrs. Ward and I shall have our revenge on you for deserting us, for you will then have the agony of the servant-girl problem on your own hands and know how it is from the other side of the house."

"Perhaps that is one of the reasons I am going to have a home of my own, Mr. Ward. I shall be able to see the question from both standpoints."

"I hope you'll be spared our troubles," Mr. Ward spoke in a really serious tone this time. Then he added with great heartiness: "The Lord bless you, Barbara. You have been like a daughter to us." He choked as he remembered Carl in Barbara's arms just a little before he passed over. "We shall miss you dreadfully. But we shall bid you God-speed. I don't know what the rest of Marble Square Church will do but you know that Mrs. Ward and myself will be loyal to our minister's wife."

"Oh, I thank you Mr. Ward. It means everything to me," and Barbara retired somewhat hastily to the kitchen, where some tears of joy and feeling dropped on the familiar old table where Carl had so often sat watching her at work.

That evening Mr. Morton called. Barbara had finished her work, and was sitting with the family as her custom was, when Morton came in.

There was a little embarrassment at the first greeting with the Wards, but it soon passed off and in a few moments the young minister was chatting delightfully. His happiness was on his face and in his manner. He had never looked so noble or so handsome, Barbara's heart said to herself, almost wondering whether it was all a dream from which she would soon be rudely awakened. But it was no dream like that. Her heart sang and she began to realize its reality.

"Oh, by the way," Mr. Ward said suddenly, turning to his wife, "Martha, how about that rule that we made long ago, that the hired girl should receive her company in the kitchen? Why did I go to all that expense of furnishing that new kitchen if the girl is going to sit here in the parlor?"

Mr. Morton jumped to his feet, and walked over to Barbara.

"Come, Barbara," he said with a touch of humor that equaled the occasion. "Come out into the kitchen where we belong. This is no place for us."

Barbara rose, blushing and laughing.

"Yes, I see. Just an excuse to get rid of us," Mr. Ward said as the lovers walked out.

"We want to live up to the rule of the house," Mr. Morton retorted.

They went out into the room where Barbara had spent so many hours of hard toil and, when they were alone, the minister said: "Dear, do you know, this room is a sacred spot to me? I have thought of you as being here more than anywhere else."

"If I had known that," Barbara said gently, and she no longer avoided the loving brown eyes that looked down on her, "it would have lightened a good many weary hours. I feel ashamed now to think of the quantities of tears I have shed in this little room."

"The thought that your life has gone out in service here, Barbara, is a beautiful thought to me. What a wonderful thing it is to be of use in the world! I thank God my mother brought me up to reverence the labor of the hand in honest toil. There is nothing more sacred in all of human life."

Then they talked of their love for each other, and were really startled when the door suddenly opened and Mr. Ward called out from the entry: "Gas and coal come high this winter. You can draw your own inference."

They rose laughing, and came back into the parlor, where Mrs. Ward apologized for Mr. Ward's interruption.

"Don't say a word, Mrs. Ward," Morton said merrily. "I shall soon have Barbara all to myself."

"How soon?"

"I don't know quite." Mr. Morton looked at Barbara.

"There will be a mourning in this household when she goes," Mrs. Ward replied. "I never expect to have another girl like Barbara."

"I'm sorry for you, but you can't expect me to feel any sorrow for myself."

"Yes, that's it," Mr. Ward put it ironically. "You preachers are always talking about sacrifice, and giving up, and all that. I notice that, when it comes to a personal application, you are just as grasping after the best there is, as anybody."

"Of course," said Morton cheerfully, looking at Barbara.

"He is going to suffer for it, though." Barbara came to the rescue of Mr. Ward. "He may lose his church just as you are going to lose me."

"I don't think so," Morton answered calmly. "But if I do –" He did not finish, but his look at Barbara spoke volumes. It said that he had found something which would compensate for any earthly loss.

When Morton had gone, Barbara slipped up to her room. Her happiness was too great to be talked about. The thought of what her lover, her "lover," she repeated, had said about service, about the image of herself daily in that kitchen, made her tremble. She had tried to accustom herself to the thought of Christ's teaching about service. Her study of the different passages in the Bible referring to servants had given her new life on the subject. It had all grown sweeter and more noble as she went on. And, now that her life had been caught up into this other life, a newer and clearer revelation of labor and ministry had come to her. Never had Barbara offered a true prayer of thanksgiving than the one that flowed out of her heart to God tonight. Never had the depth and beauty of human service meant so much to her as now, when human love, the love sanctioned by Jesus and made holy by His benediction, had begun to translate common things into divine terms.

In her Bible-reading that night she found a passage in the sixth chapter of Second Corinthians that pleased her very much. It did not belong first of all to the service of a house-servant; yet Barbara felt quite sure, as she read, that if Paul had been questioned about it, he would have said that the teaching applied just as well to house-ministration as to ministration elsewhere. This is the passage which she read:

"Giving no offence in any thing, that the ministry be not blamed: But in all things approving ourselves as the ministers of God, in much patience, in afflictions, in necessities, in distresses, In stripes, in imprisonments, in tumults, in labours, in watchings, in fastings; By pureness, by knowledge, by longsuffering, by kindness, by the Holy Ghost, by love unfeigned, By the word of truth, by the power of God, by the armour of righteousness on the right hand and on the left, By honour and dishonor, by evil report and good report: as deceivers, and yet true; As unknown, and yet well known; as dying, and, behold, we live; as chastened, and not killed; As sorrowful, yet always rejoicing; as poor, yet making many rich; as having nothing, and yet possessing all things." (II Corinthians 6:3-10)

"Have I been a 'minister of God?' How often I have complained and shed tears over little things as I have tried to minister to the needs of this house! Surely at its very worst I have not endured the hardships that Paul speaks of. I know he is speaking of preachers, probably, of missionaries of the cross. But I am sure he means that anyone who 'ministers' to the real needs of life is a 'minister of God.' And, if I have really been a minister of God, how little I have realized its meaning!"

"Help me, my Father," Barbara breathed her prayer, "help me in the thankfulness for the great joy of my life to live as a servant of Thine. Through all these possible hardships may I learn to keep close to Thee. Help me to bless other lives and give them encouragement and a true thought of ministry. It is all so wonderful, my Father! Thou hast led me in ways so unforeseen by my poor selfishness. It is all too wonderful to me. Oh Thou Great but loving God, I thank Thee. In the name of Him who has redeemed me. Amen."

It was the next day that Barbara had a call from Mrs. Vane.

The old lady had met Mr. Morton; and reading his happiness in his whole person, she asked him bluntly to tell her about it.

"My dear," she cried as she kissed Barbara on both cheeks and shed a tear out of her sharp eyes, softened by her love for Barbara, "I congratulate you both! It is wonderful; but I knew all the time that he loved you and would have you and I knew that you would give yourself to him. It is all as it should be. The Marble Square Church is a great institution, but it is not so great as love. I want you to be married at my house. Morton is one of my boys. I knew him as a child, and I love him as a son."

"I don't think mother would allow me to go away from her, even to you," Barbara answered, smiling and blushing until she looked like a picture, Mrs. Vane and Mrs. Ward both thought as they stood looking at her. "We have arranged to be married at mother's."

"That's best; yes, that's best!" The old lady nodded approvingly. "No church display, no show, no cheap or vulgar flaunting of self on the occasion of the most sacred experience in a girl's life. I always said Ralph Morton deserved the best woman on earth for a wife and he's getting her. The good God bless you both!" And the impulsive old lady kissed Barbara again; and, when Barbara went back to her work she remained some time with Mrs. Ward, talking over the great event; for it was truly great to Barbara and Morton and his friends, and indeed to all Marble Square parish.

For, when the news of the minister's engagement became known in Crawford, as it did in a very short time, because he made no secret of it, there was consternation in Marble Square Church and in society generally.

"Is it true?" Mrs. Rice solemnly asked Mrs. Wilson the first time they met after the news became known, "is it really true that Mr. Morton is going to marry Mrs. Ward's hired girl? It is simply awful. It cannot be."

"I'm afraid it is," Mrs. Wilson answered, clasping her hands with a tragic gesture as if some terrible calamity had taken place. "I had the information direct from Mrs. Vane, who had it direct from Mr. Morton himself."

"It will break up Marble Square Church, that is all!" Mrs. Rice said decidedly. "A thing like that is too serious a social departure for even Mr. Morton to make. As much as people like and admire him, not even his great talents can excuse such a great social blunder."

"They say," Mrs. Wilson suggested in a hesitating manner, "that the girl is really well educated, and not just an ordinary hired girl. You know Mrs. Ward has told us something about her going out to service in order to help other girls realize its dignity and – and so forth."

"It makes no difference!" Mrs. Rice replied sharply. "She is known as a hired girl. The idea of being obliged to look up to her as our minister's wife! Will you submit to that?"

"Supposing she proves worthy of her place?" Mrs. Wilson suggested feebly.

"It's out of the question!" Mrs. Rice answered positively. "The whole thing is awfully unfortunate for Marble Square. If Mr. Morton had only chosen some girl of good social rank, Miss Dillingham, for example. But, as it is, I for one –"

Mrs. Rice did not finish what seemed like a threat, but scores of other women in Marble Square felt and spoke just as she did, and the outlook for a great disturbance in the parish was very great.

When Sunday came, Barbara prepared to attend service. She had not been for several Sundays, not since the time of the scene at the Endeavor Society. Mrs. Ward wondered at her lack of nervousness. There was a self-possession about Barbara, now that she had committed her future to the young minister, that Mrs. Ward admired. She began to have a real respect for her in addition to her affection.

When Barbara went down the aisle with the family and entered the Ward pew with the rest, it is safe to say that every eye in Marble Square church was directed toward her. What people saw, very many of them to their great surprise, was a lovely face, free from affectation or superficial prettiness, without bashful consciousness of her prominent position. Every woman in the house could not help acknowledging, "She looks like a lady." Love had done much for Barbara. It is a wonderful power to dignify and bless.

There were hundreds of people in Marble Square Church that morning who had just come from the perusal of one of Crawford's most sensational Sunday papers, which with cruelty and a coarseness that was actually criminal, had printed what it called, in staring headlines, "A Spicy Tale of a Hired Girl and a Preacher. The Rev. Mr. Morton, of the Fashionable Marble Square Church, To Wed a Hired Girl. Full Particulars of the Engagement. With Snap-Shots of the Parties." There were two columns of description that were worthy of authorship form the lowest pit, accompanied with what purported to be reliable pictures of the two lovers. And it was from the perusal of all this horrible invasion of every sacred and tender private feeling that the human heart holds dear, that most of the men and women had come into church that morning to add to the sensation by almost as heartless and cruel a scrutiny of Barbara and Mr. Morton.

Barbara did not know all of this; but, even if she had, her love was so pure and great that it is doubtful whether anything could have obscured her perfect happiness. When her lover rose to preach, she never felt more pride in him, or more confidence in his powers.

He fully justified all her expectations. Unlike Barbara, he knew quite fully all the venom and vileness of the paper in question. On his way to church, grinning newsboys had flaunted the pages in his face and shouted their contents in his ears. From all that, he had gone into his room, and after the sustaining prayer that had refreshed and quieted his soul he had gone out to face the people. But he had first faced God. He was not in the least afraid of the people after that.

It is doubtful whether Marble Square Church had ever heard such preaching before. It is doubtful whether Morton had ever before had such a vision or delivered such a message. The power was over the great congregation. Hearts that had come to criticize, to sneer, to ridicule, were touched by his words. Members of his parish who after reading the paper had fully made up their minds to sever all connection with the church changed their minds during the wonderfully sweet and helpful prayer that followed the sermon. Ah, Barbara and Ralph! The Spirit of God is greater than all the evil of men. If victory comes out of all this suffering for you, it will be due to God's power over the selfish, thoughtless, cruel children of men.

When the service was over, Barbara quietly went out with Mrs. Ward. In the vestibule they were met by Mrs. Dillingham, who had come out of the other door from a side aisle.

With scores of people noting what was said and done the majestic old lady greeted Barbara with a courteous and even kindly greeting that was unmistakable and created a genuine sensation, for no family in all Marble Square Church had higher connections than the Dillinghams.

"My dear Miss Clark," Mrs. Dillingham had said, "your mother was kind enough to return my call. You have not been so good. Will you come and see me soon?"

"Indeed I will, Mrs. Dillingham, if you have forgiven my neglect of your invitation so far."

"I'll forgive anything in a Dillingham. You don't forget you're one of us as I have said before."

She swept out of the vestibule grandly, holding her head a little higher than usual, and Barbara blessed the nobility in her that was unspoiled by all her riches and social rank. Probably nothing that occurred that morning made a deeper impression socially. The old lady had not said a word about the engagement. She had too much delicacy and good taste. But it was just as plain as if she had welcomed Barbara as her minister's wife that she accepted the situation without a thought of remonstrance and was prepared to act loyally towards Mr. Morton, respecting his choice and even ready to defend it before any and all of her influential acquaintances.

Miss Dillingham was at the other end of the vestibule while her mother was talking to Barbara. She did not approach Barbara, and, so far as could be seen, did not even look at her during the service. Her proud, handsome face was directed, however, with a fixed and painful gaze upon the preacher through all the service. If at the close Alice Dillingham calmly shut the door of her own heart over its dream of romance in which the talented preacher of Marble Square had begun to be adored, it may be that Barbara fully understood it; and in avoidance of her by the one who had lost what Barbara had gained, Barbara saw no cause for personal ill will. When the heart aches, there are times when it must ache alone, and riches and beauty are no security and no comfort.

The weeks that followed this eventful Sunday were crowded with incidents and meaning for Barbara. She remained nearly a month with Mrs. Ward, until help had been secured, and then with mutual sorrow the women parted, Barbara going home to make preparation, with her mother's help, for her marriage.

'If you aren't suited with the situation you've found, you can come back to us any time," Mr. Ward said as his wife kissed Barbara and made no attempt to hide her sorrow plainly shown by the tears on her face.

"Thank you," responded Barbara, laughing through her tears, for it was a real grief for her to go; "I am afraid I shall never come back. But, if you will come and see us, I will promise to bake some of your favorite dishes for you."

She waved her hand to them as they both came to the door and bade her an affectionate farewell, and soon turned the corner, with a grave consciousness that one very important chapter in her life had come to a close and a new one had begun.

Three months after, Barbara was married at her mother's home. The few friends who had been faithful to her during the days of her service were present, the Wards, Mr. and Mrs. Vane, and Mrs. Dillingham, together with three of the girls from the stores whose friendship for Barbara had daily grown in meaning. A seminary classmate of Morton's spoke the words of the service in which God joined these two eager, earnest Christian souls in one, and they twain became one flesh, and another home was added to those that already on the earth are the best witness to the possibilities of heaven among men.

Five years after this, Barbara and her husband were standing together one evening in the dining-room of the parsonage of Marble Square Church, evidently awaiting some guests.

Ralph Morton was nodding approval of some little detail of the table furnishing, and Barbara was saying, "So lovely to have the old friends with us tonight, isn't it, Ralph?"

"Indeed it is. Although I could be satisfied with present company," the minister answered gallantly. He was still the lover as well as husband.

"That's selfish." Barbara smiled as she came around to his side of the table and stood there with his arm about her, the love light in her eyes as strong as ever.

"I have never quite got over that interruption of Mr. Ward's the night I courted you in your kitchen," he said, laughing.

"You have had five years to make it up, sir," Barbara replied, answering his laugh with a caress, and as the bell rang she ran to the door to meet her guests.

"We've all come along together, you see," Mr. Ward said in his cheery fashion as he entered with Mrs. Ward and Mr. and Mrs. Vane and Mrs. Dillingham. "We have been over to the training school and looked at the new addition. It's a great help."

The minister and his wife greeted them eagerly; and, when they were seated at the table, after grace was asked the talk naturally turned about the work of the training-school and its results. A neat-looking girl with a pleasant, intelligent face came in to serve the first course.

"Jennie," Barbara said, with a smile that revealed her winsomeness, and proved that the years had added to its power, "these are old friends of mine. You have met Mrs. Ward, Mrs. Dillingham, Mr. and Mrs. Vane, Jennie Mason."

The girl nodded pleasantly in response to the words of greeting given her, and when her work was over she went out.

"Is Miss Mason one of your girls?" Mrs. Vane asked, rubbing her nose vigorously as her wont was when she had some particular problem in mind.

"Yes, she is just out of the school. She is really fitting herself for hospital service, but wanted to take the course, and is with me this winter."

"Are these her muffins?" Mr. Ward inquired suspiciously.

"No, sir," Barbara laughed. "Those are mine. I made them specially for you in memory of the old times."

"Ah, we've never had any like them since you left us for a better place, have we, Martha?" Mr. Ward said, turning to his wife.

"No, not even the girls from Barbara's school can equal her," Mrs. Ward answered, giving Barbara a grateful look. The years had strengthened their friendship and love.

"I don't see that the training-school has solved the hired-girl problem in Crawford," Mrs. Vane said as if vexed at something she had heard. "Although it is wonderful what has been done in so short a time."

"We've had our woes," Barbara answered with a sigh. "It takes so long to make people see the divine side of service. Now, Jennie, as good and capable a girl as she is, longs to escape the drudgery as she calls it, and become something besides a servant."

"As long as humanity is what it is, I imagine that will always keep the problem unsolved. But I am sure the girls who go out of the school are learning the beauty of service more and more every year."

"I can speak for the truth of that," Mrs. Dillingham nodded vigorously to Barbara across the table. "The girl you sent me last week is a treasure. She is neat, competent, and Christian. I am ready to pay her the maximum wages at the start."

Mrs. Dillingham referred to a scale of wages agreed upon in Crawford since the training-school was started. This scale was a mutual agreement between housekeepers and servants, and was regulated by certain well-defined conditions of competency. It provided for a certain increase every month of a small amount, and had proved mutually helpful as far as tried.

"At the same time," Mrs. Ward said, "I don't believe the servant-girl problem is mostly one of wages or work. I believe it is more a question or an understanding on the part of those who go out to service of the opportunity to serve, and the real joy of being in a place where one is really needed by the homes of the world."

"Hear! Hear!" cried Mr. Vane, who was an unusually modest man and seldom took any extended part in the talk. "That's what Mrs. Morton has always preached, if I understand her."

"Indeed, yes!" Barbara answered, her eyes flashing with enthusiasm. "All we have done so far in the training-school has been to make an honest effort to teach girls to be competent in the affairs of the house so far as its management is concerned, and after doing that comes the hardest part of it – to help the girls to see the divine side of service. That is particularly hard to teach, especially if, as in the case of several of our best girls, they have suffered injustice and un-Christian treatment from so-called Christian women. That is still my greatest problem. I think I could soon furnish all the competent help that Crawford needs if housekeepers would do their part to solve the difficulties, just as you helped me," Barbara added, turning to Mrs. Ward and Mrs. Vane.

She was going on to add a word more to the little "preachment," as Mr. Morton called it, when the company was startled by the appearance of a little figure in white, which had stolen down the stairs and suddenly appeared in the dining-room.

"Why don't I have any of this?" the figure said reproachfully, and everybody laughed while the child ran around to Barbara and put a curly head in her lap.

"Now, then, little boys that are put to bed must stay there," Barbara said, smiling at the sweet face that looked up at her after the first moment.

"Can't I stay and have some?" the child asked, pleading a little. "I dreamed you were having some good things without me, and I thought you would miss me; and – and – so – I came down."

Barbara hesitated and looked over at the father. Ralph's lip trembled suspiciously, but he said quite gently, but firmly: "No, Carl, you must go right back to bed. It is too late for little boys to be up. We are very much obliged for your call, but we cannot ask you to stay."

"All right," said Carl sturdily. He raised his face to his mother's, and kissed her, and marched sturdily out of the room. At the door he fired a parting shot.

"If there's anything left, save Martha and me some."

He vanished up the stairs amid a general laugh, and Mrs. Ward wiped her eyes. It was more than laughter that had brought tears to them.

"I think you have the most beautiful children, Barbara. I never saw any that minded like your Carl."

"I'm afraid they obey their father better than me," Barbara answered slowly. "But they are lovely children. Did you ever see anything more funny than the look on his face as he said, 'Why don't I have some of this?' And as for Martha –" Barbara's eyes dimmed at the vision of that little one upstairs; and, when she came back to the conversation Mr. Ward was saying: "That was a trying time, Barbara. I tell you now, that I had no sort of expectation that you could hold your own in Marble Square. The night you were married I knew there were a dozen families fully intending to leave the church and never come back."

"And yet they didn't. At least, not more than two or three. How do you account for it?" Mrs. Vane asked the question, and then answered it herself. "Plain enough. They learned to love the minister's wife."

"Same's I did," said Ralph, bowing to Barbara. "I knew I was safe all the time."

"But there are some people that never have called on you yet, my dear?" Mrs. Dillingham asked.

144

"Yes, quite a number," Barbara answered quietly. "It does not hurt me. I am very happy."

The little company was silent a moment. Each was tracing in memory some of the eventful things of the last five years.

"It is a great work you and Mr. Morton have done," Mrs. Ward said at last. "When you came into my house, Barbara, six years ago, I was a fretful, irritable, cross woman. Your definition of Christian service really saved our home. What you are doing for other girls in training them to have a divine thought of service is saving many other homes in Crawford. I know it because I see the effects on my friends wherever your girls have gone. You will never know, Barbara, all the good you have done amongst us."

"God has been very good to me," said Barbara softly.

"He has been good to us all," her husband added gently.

After supper Barbara went upstairs to see her mother and say good-night to her. Mrs. Clark had for two years been confined to her room through an accident. This was one of the cheerful burdens that Barbara had carried since her home began. She stayed with her mother for some time, and Ralph came up and joined her with Mrs. Ward, until the invalid ordered them all downstairs again.

"The children are company for me," she said, and Barbara's tears fell as she said to Mrs. Ward, "I do believe mother is glad that she is one of the 'shut-ins.' She does enjoy Carl and Martha so! They play together all the time, and even when they are asleep mother calls them company." She kissed her mother good-night and joined the company downstairs.

"Oh, did I tell you?" she said as she came down. "Ralph and I invited a little group of friends among the young people tonight. They'll be here pretty soon."

"We hope they're from a class of society that is equal to ours, Barbara," said Mr. Ward gravely. "The last time I was here, Morton introduced me to a lot of people who work with their hands in making an honest living. That isn't the 'best society' you know in Crawford."

Barbara looked at him humorously.

"Remarks like that do not frighten me any more," she said. "The 'best society' to me is made up of people who have begun to learn the lesson of divine service for human needs."

The young people arrived a little later. They were young men and women whom Ralph and Barbara had met and drawn into the circle of their companionship in service. There were eight or ten girls who were out at service, and had been trained in the school as Barbara's own pupils. There were three or four girls from Bondman's, who were trying to live in little apartments, in one or two cases, to Barbara's own knowledge, in terrible danger of losing their virtue on account of their surroundings.

The careless-looking girl was there, the one whom Barbara had actually saved from the pit; and with the light of life in her transformed face she was living a useful life as manager of a temperance restaurant in the city. She was engaged to one of the clerks in Bondman's, and they were to be married soon and begin a little business of their own in connection with the Restaurant. As Barbara watched them talking together with her husband, she said to herself, "It is worth all it cost to save her," and only God and Barbara will ever know how much it cost and they will never tell.

Then there were half a dozen young men from various places in the city, all of whom had no homes and had been saved by Morton from an aimless or sinful life. Nearly all of the young people were among the wage-earners.

There were light refreshments passed after an evening of animated talk interspersed with much good music and several games, in which Mr. Morton surprised even Barbara with his good spirit and an ability like genius in setting everybody at ease.

About ten o'clock the minister called the guests' attention to the hour, and said quietly, "We'll have our usual service to close with."

Most of them seemed familiar with the custom at the parsonage, and the company was soon quietly seated in the two large rooms.

Ralph turned to Matthew's Gospel, and read the passage in which Jesus Christ, the Son of God, defines the term "brotherhood."

"While he yet talked to the people, behold, his mother and his brethren stood without, desiring to speak with him. Then one said unto him, Behold, thy mother and thy brethren stand without, desiring to speak with thee. But he answered and said unto him that told him, Who is my mother? and who are my brethren? And he stretched forth his hand toward his disciples, and said, Behold my mother and my brethren! For whosoever shall do the will of my Father which is in heaven, the same is my brother, and sister, and mother." (Matthew 12:46 – 50)

He commented on it briefly, and then read the other passage which contains the matchless statement of service as given by Jesus again, – "For even the Son of man came not to be ministered unto, but to minister, and to give his life a ransom for many." (Mark 10:45)

"The world will solve all hard questions if it only brings enough love to bear upon them," he said, looking out earnestly at the silent, eager young life in the circle. "Love can do all things. If only we learn that service is divine, we can learn how to make a better world and redeem our brothers and sisters."

He offered a brief prayer that the Father would bless all the lives present and all dear to them, and give them strength for another day's work after a night's peaceful rest; and after the prayer the guests quietly went away after a strong hand-shake and hearty 'God bless you' from the young preacher and his wife. Ah, Ralph and Barbara, only the judgment will reveal the number of jewels in your crown. For you have saved souls from death here and despair hereafter.

When Mrs. Dillingham went out, as she walked along with Mrs. Vane and the Wards, for they lived only a short distance from the parsonage, she said: "Well, there was a time when no one could have made me believe in the sort of evening I have spent tonight. I rubbed my eyes several times, thinking maybe I was resurrected, living in another world."

"I don't think the millennium has come quite yet," said Mrs. Ward, "not even in Crawford. And yet Barbara and Morton seem to have made a little one of their own around them."

"Perhaps that's the way the big one is going to begin," suggested Mrs. Vane wisely.

When all the people had gone, Ralph Morton and Barbara reviewed the evening.

"They had a good time, I am sure. It's worth while isn't it, dear?"

"Yes, even if I haven't solved the servant-girl problem like a mathematical thing with an exact answer," Barbara said, smiling.

"Human problems are not solved that way, Barbara. I always feel suspicious of an economic formula that claims to bring the millennium like an express-train running on a schedule time. But this much we do know from our own experience: "Love is the great solution, the final solution, of all earth's troubles. We know it is, because God is love. And service between man and man will be what it ought to be when love among men is what it ought to be, and not until then."

"I am glad," said Barbara, "that we have learned that. I am glad that we were born to serve."

"Amen," said Morton gently. "Thanks be to God for the Servant of the human race."

So hand in hand these two, through their church and home, are ministering today to the needy of the brotherhood. Hand in hand they look with the hope of God for the dawn of a better day and the victory which always crowns the greatest of all human forces, the love of man for others.

~THE END ~

Appendix

(Bonus Story)

Painting by American Artist, Daniel Ridgway Knight, 1895

"Memory and Hope Walking Along the Highway"

The following story was written in 1909. It was gleaned from the pages of "A Charles M. Sheldon Yearbook." It offers help and encouragement.

Ask yourself this question: On your life journey, are you (going backwards) like "Memory" or (cheerfully going forward) as "Hope"?

                                           ꙮ ꙮ ꙮ ꙮ ꙮ ꙮ ꙮ ꙮ

Memory and Hope met each other once as they were going along life's highway, and stopped to exchange greetings. Hope was walking with elastic step and serene brow. Memory had her eyes pensively fixed upon the ground, and walked slowly and with frequent pauses.

"Good morning," said Hope cheerfully. "Whither art thou going?"

"Back over the way I came," replied Memory.

"Art thou not weary going over the old path?"

"At times I am, but there are many scenes I love to revisit."

"On the whole, however," said Hope, "it seems to me thy traveling companions are many of them, at best, troublesome and even exceedingly sorrowful. I wish thou wert not going the backward way. Wilt thou not join us? All the saints are going our way. All the army of the redeemed who have washed their robes white in the blood of the Lamb are going with me over the road. It is good company; the best in life."

But I saw Memory shake her head, and continue sadly on her way; and Hope, with no time to waste in useless regrets, prepared to advance.

Then I, who had been hesitating between Memory and Hope, came up to Hope and said: "May I join thee? Hast thou room for me in thy company?"

"And who art thou?" asked Hope gently.

"A human soul," I answered sadly; "one buffeted with trouble, beset by doubts, cast down by loss, terrified at the thought of death, and in great need of comfort."

Then Hope held out the hand and drew me along the way with her, saying joyously: "Welcome, Oh soul of Humanity! Come! Thou shalt walk with me up to the Pearly Gates. Forget thou the things that are behind and stretch forward with me unto the things that are before."

So I let Hope lead me along the way; and when night came, Faith and Love joined us, and we journeyed on through the night, which shone even in the darkness with the star-lamps of heaven.

And in the darkest places of all I heard Hope singing, singing as if God had taught her, singing in an undertone: "It is better farther on."

- Charles M. Sheldon.

About the Author

Portrait from "A Charles M. Sheldon Yearbook," 1909.

Charles M. Sheldon (1857 – 1946), the son of a minister, was born in New York.

He graduated from Andover Theological Seminary in 1886. At the age of 29 he started preaching at a country church in Vermont. Two years later he was called to be the pastor of Central Church in Topeka, Kansas, where he served until 1919.

He and his wife, Mary, were the parents of one child. He was a Lecturer, Writer, and Preacher. He is most known for his best-selling book, "In His Steps." The book was published in 1897 and has sold millions of copies.

[This information was gathered from his autobiography, published in 1925.]

For more titles by The Legacy of Home Press, please visit us at:

https://thelegacyofhomepress.blogspot.com

Made in the USA
Middletown, DE
28 February 2023

25883452R00092